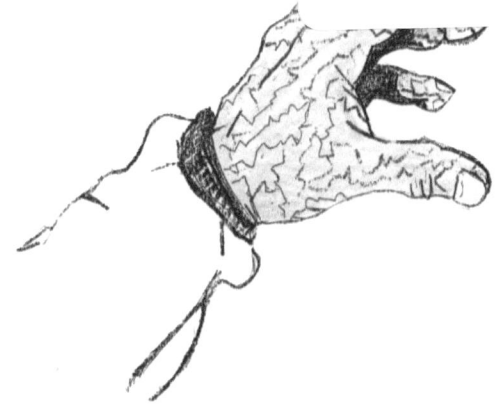

THE MAN WITH THE ELECTRIC ARM

BY
BUDD STEADMAN

EDITED BY:
JOE MALACINA

No Limit Enterprises, Inc. | Chicago, IL

The Man with the Electric Arm

No Limit Enterprises, Inc.
www.nolimitcorp.com

Text and Illustrations © 2022 by No Limit Enterprises, Inc.

For additional information, contact the publisher: No Limit Enterprises, Inc., 503 Sagebrush Ct., Lake Villa, IL 60046, United States or via www.nolimitcorp.com.

The Man with the Electric Arm
1st Edition
Author: Budd Steadman
Co-Author & Editor: Joe Malacina
Editors: Gary Yambor & Camaryn Sapienza
Cover Design by: Kayla Schweisberger
ISBN: 979-8-9858398-4-5
Library of Congress Control Number: 2022937160
Published in Chicago, IL, USA

To the entire Steadman family, and the many more influenced by the legacy of Budd Steadman.

CONTENTS

CHAPTER 1 - THE STORM   9

CHAPTER 2 - A PHENOMENOM IN SURVIVAL   13

CHAPTER 3 - THE INTRUDERS   19

CHAPTER 4 - CATASTROPHE   27

CHAPTER 5 - A JOURNEY BEGINS   35

CHAPTER 6 - THE CONFRONTATION   59

CHAPTER 7 - A JOURNEY FULFILLED   73

CHAPTER 8 - KEEPING A PROMISE   85

CHAPTER 9 - THE UNEXPECTED   99

CHAPTER 10 - AGAINST THE ODDS   119

CHAPTER 11 - THE CRITICAL HOURS   127

CHAPTER 12 - TAKING TO THE ROAD AGAIN   131

CHAPTER 13 - THE DESERT ORDEAL   149

CHAPTER 14 - ESCAPE TO NOWHERE   159

CHAPTER 15 - HONORING A PROMISE   171

CHAPTER 16 - THE AGONY OF PURSUIT   185

CHAPTER 17 - A BLUEPRINT FOR SURVIVAL   201

CHAPTER 18 - DESPERATE HOURS   211

CHAPTER 19 - A JOURNEY INTO OBLIVION   219

THE MAN WITH THE ELECTRIC ARM

CHAPTER 1
THE STORM

Few residents living throughout the scenic high country of the Sierra Madres could recall such a fierce storm. Constant lightning crackled across the black tortured sky. Explosions of thunder echoed against the high walls, and heavy rain cascaded in thumping sounds against the rugged mountains. The vast landscape reverberated with roaring rivers and twisted falling timbers.

Incredibly, like tiny spiders clinging to a disintegrating web, two California Electric Company linemen doggedly performed their precarious repair duties atop a spindly high-tension tower. At fourteen thousand feet, Peter Lipton and his partner Zakaria worked furiously through the tormented night, in an attempt to stave the severed wires of the high-tension spire. Their objective now was to concentrate on renewing service to the blackouts of hospitals and other emergency facilities within the mountainous perimeter.

They had worked nonstop throughout the night and into the early dawn hours. Lightning flashes reflected their glistening yellow rubberized coveralls. Working no more than five feet apart, their perilous positions resembled a circus high-wire team embarking on a death-defying feat. Only this performance, minus a net, was more treacherous and spectacular.

Dangling from their steel perch and yelling through the noise of the pummeling rain to communicate, Peter and Zak steadfastly persevered. Gasping, Peter yelled, "Zak, I think we'll have to forget this final leg of the chain. We're pushing the envelope now old pal, so I say we run for cover in the truck while we still can. Let's get some sleep and maybe start again in the morning. What do you say, Zak?"

Steady lightning flashes cast an ominous glow across the shadowy hooded face of Zak. A look of steel resolve lined his determined mouth. "Ten minutes more Peter and we can ditch this big top," he shouted.

Peter persisted, his words coming in short spurts, "Zak, these wires are impossible to control, and this lightning and rain aren't letting up. Look down Zak, that's like looking through death's tunnel. I tell you, man, let's get our butts out of here now!"

Without reply, Zak's familiar determined grimace told the intent of the man many fellow workers considered uniquely different.

CHAPTER 1

Yelling, Peter Lipton began to climb down within the huge jigsaw steel superstructure. "You stay if you want Zak, I'm getting out of here. I've had it."

Zak only glanced at Peter, his sculptured nose protruding from the yellow hood, his deep-set eyes reflecting streaks of lightning. Turning away, he resumed his task, determined to complete the high road demands. Suddenly, an immense lightning bolt blinded their senses. The huge tower structure they were working on shuddered, then, in slow motion, avalanched downward and miraculously jolted to a halt.

Both hapless figures were ripped from their positions, falling crazily through the metallic cobweb. Zak's quick instincts helped him wrap his arm around an electrified steel bar as it blurred past. Lightning allowed a flashbulb-view of his partner Peter, his doomed body ricocheting off the steel beams and plummeting downward into oblivion, engulfed by the rage of nature's fury.

Desperately straining to pull himself over the still flickering beam, Zak winced at the obvious futility. Another lightning surge struck, and the entire tower structure sparkled like a burning Christmas tree. Momentarily, the gangling electrified derrick held as though frozen, then brightened even more before it crumpled into domino form. Drowned in a fireball of an iridescent splash, the obliterated tower fell, diving toward the bottomless pit of the jagged valley below…

Morning's dead silence throughout the Sierras seemed lacking in contrast to the ferocity of the night before. Slowly, the sweet songs of birds welcoming the new day broke the stillness. Rivers flowed gently and placid lakes mirrored a look of contentment. Only a patchwork of twisted branches and fallen trees floating along the smooth water gave evidence to the fury of the long night before.

Reports of emergencies throughout the Sierras flooded the official Forest Ranger Headquarters. Included in the many crisis messages was a mention of three fallen high-tension towers and the possible tragic involvement of two California linemen, missing somewhere along the Big Spur Ridge. Their abandoned utility truck had been discovered in a heavy mudslide at the low ground near the raging Snake River.

CHAPTER 2
A PHENOMENOM IN
SURVIVAL

The overflowing Snake River maintained its fast current, rippling through turbulent rapids and deafening waterfalls. Countless fallen trees and underbrush whirled along its embattled surface.

At a severe turn in the river's course, the flow temporarily abated, creating a jam of crammed debris. Within the flow of the maze, an unnaturally bright yellow color glistened from the rubberized sleeve of a rain garment.

The man called Zak clung fiercely to a shamble of timber, sporadically gasping for air. Entangled within the forest's swamp-like refuse, his body soon became wedged close to the shore.

In final desperation, Zak reached out both arms and clawed to pull himself to the shore; then he succumbed to the darkness of unconsciousness.

Most of the day passed into early evening as a partial moon and its light blanketed the ravaged terrain. Search parties continued to scour the impenetrable treachery of the great Sierras. The charred and mutilated body of Peter Lipton had been found floating in the Snake River. His body had drifted downstream, over fifty miles from where he last reported his position by phone to the electric company. Peter's partner, although assumed dead, had yet to be recovered, and for legal reasons, his name was still being withheld from the public.

Downriver, the naturally inquisitive nose of a large, grizzled muskrat sniffed warily at the strange bright yellow form at the water's edge. Deciding to investigate the soft and tempting texture it had discovered, the grubbing animal dug its teeth into the arm of the stilled, dilapidated figure.

There came a faint crackling sound and smoke arose, the muskrat's body shook, then stiffened, as the life was sucked out of it. The rodent's body smoldered, and a pungent stench of burnt fur permeated the air around it.

Unmoving, the lifeless body of Zak lay in the muck while the dawn of another day approached.

"Scrappy, Scrappy girl, what the hell are you hunting up now?" echoed a graveled voice near the river's edge. Sam Rooney, a legendary gold prospector known throughout the high country, scrambled from the thorny underbrush.

CHAPTER 2

His hound dog, Scrappy, had come upon the rag-tailed body of the missing California lineman, Zak. Still, no movement could be detected as Sam Rooney knelt over the prostrate, tattered figure.

"Dang, if this ain't a man, or what's left of him. Sure ain't never seen such a mess of anyone in all my born days." It was then that Sam noticed the burnt remains of a muskrat lying along the side of the motionless man's arm. Focusing now on the arm, he observed a gash and what looked like a burn mark running down the entire length.

Sam shook his head, "Scrappy, you old buzzard, grab hold with your teeth and help me drag this big bag of bones from the water."

With the help of the large dog, Sam managed to move the disheveled body to dry ground. "God almighty if he ain't got a pulse, and a slight heartbeat," he exclaimed, checking for signs of life. Now, on dry ground, Sam was able to finally get a good look at the body that lay before him. What he saw shocked him.

"Whatever happened to this character sure pulverized his face. Wonder what he really looked like. Right now, he'd scare a dog off a meat truck Scrappy. A plastic surgeon I ain't, but whatever first aid I have in my sack might stop the bleeding and bring down some of the swelling."

While continuing to carry on a one-way conversation with his dog Scrappy, Sam Rooney hastily constructed a lean-to, built a fire, and covered Zak in the one blanket he carried.

"Scrappy, I can't believe this guy has no broken bones. For sure he's got a lot of intestinal fortitude and he's going to need more. I figure we have to get him off the wet ground and into the shack. That means you stay here, buddy, while I bring back Mule and more blankets." Mule being his faithful donkey, whom he named Mule because he believed only people should be called "Jackass."

Another day had passed before Sam returned with the pack mule and supplies. No change could be seen in the condition of his unconscious patient. The dog Scrappy sat alongside the innate figure, as though guarding her shattered, befriended stranger.

Sliding from his tired mule, Sam patted Scrappy. "Good girl, Scrap, looks like our poor partner ain't doing too well, huh? Well, if I can just lean him up against old Mule and lay him over Mule's back, we can get him to the shack."

CHAPTER 2

Using a nearby tree to brace Zak's body, Sam slowly edged the limp figure over the curved back of his staunch pack mule. "Sure ain't strong as I used to be mister," he complained, "but you're on board and in a day, we'll be inside the cabin."

The one-room cabin extended from the entrance of what was obviously an abandoned mine. A small pot-bellied stove warmed the interior. A table, a bed, a chest, and an old high-backed chair comprised the shack's furnishings.

After a laborious struggle, Sam was finally able to drag Zak's body into the cabin and onto the bed. When he attempted to turn the limp body on its side, an almost undetectable groan arose for the first time.

"Did you hear that Scrappy? He's alive alright and kicking."

Three days passed without Sam's patient gaining consciousness. Heavily covered in layers of blankets and a constant force-feeding of hot liquids brought no additional response. The stranger he had recovered at the river's edge was apparently mired in a coma.

A PHENOMENOM IN SURVIVAL

CHAPTER 3
THE INTRUDERS

Early evening arrived as Sam carefully administered another spoonful of soup through the scabbed lips of Zak. Sam spoke softly, "Your face still looks like a jigsaw puzzle mister, but the swelling is going down some. I better get a few more logs for the fire so the night will be warm in here." Scrappy followed him out the door as Sam proceeded to a nearby woodpile. Picking up a stack of logs, his dog Scrappy barked and Sam quickly turned, sensing a presence.

Standing on each side of his cabin door were two men dressed in black biker jackets, grubby jeans, and small pistols inside their belts.

"Who are you? What do you want?" Sam blurted out.

They smiled insidiously while a third similarly dressed cohort with blond pony-tailed hair came from behind the shack; he spoke. "Just taking a scenic tour through the wild country, old man. My nature-loving friends and I spotted your cabin. We thought someone in this picturesque surrounding might offer a little hospitality."

The dog began to growl and show her sizeable teeth to the strangers.

"Calm that darn dog down old man, that thing comes at me, and I'll kick its dang teeth in." Sam turned to the dog, "It's okay Scrappy, these boys ain't here to hurt us." The dog stopped growling but kept her keen eyes directly on the men.

Cradling the wood, Sam walked slowly towards the partially opened cabin door. "I ain't old, and you guys came in awful quiet, I didn't hear a thing. I'm just getting this wood for the fire and my sick friend."

"Sick friend? Maybe we can help, partner," the talkative one replied.

"Don't think so mister, my good pal is coming along, but I thank you anyway," Sam walked warily up to the door opening.

The skinny one, heavily tattooed and sprouting a stubble beard, giggled then put his arm across the doorway, blocking Sam's entrance. "Now you see, old man," said the chattering leader of the group, "it ain't very neighborly of you to just put us off like that. It's getting dark, and we've always been afraid of the boogie man. How about sharing a hot cup of tea with us?" The bikers laughed.

"Ok wise guys, what's this all about?" Sam demanded.

CHAPTER 3

The dog, ever alert, began to growl again, louder this time and began to move towards the men.

The big one, sensing the dog could be a problem, said nothing, grabbed Sam by his collar and threw him bodily into the cabin and across the floor, scattering the firewood. All three intruders rushed inside. The giggling skinny one slammed the door and placed a 2 x 4 barrier across its 'L' braces. Outside, Scrappy began to bark and claw at the door.

"Home sweet home, I always say," remarked the pony-tailed leader. "Let's cut the crap," he continued, "we're here because word has it that some old bastard named Sam has a hoard of gold from his mother load up here. Ain't that right, Sam? Reno, pick up that old fart and sit him in the chair. We got some talking to do."

The big silent one, who was busting out of his black studded jacket, plucked Sam from the floor, and crashed him into a wooden chair.

The dog continued to protest relentlessly outside the cabin.

"I don't provoke," Sam disdainfully retorted. Defiantly, he added, "That's from *For Whom the Bell Tolls*, if that makes any sense to you overgrown morons."

The leader leaned over, pushing his heavily bearded face into Sam's nose. "Old man, the bell will ring for you right now if we don't find that pile of gold, got that?" Giggling continued from the emaciated one. "And shut that darn dog up or I'll go out there and shut him up permanently."

Sam called from the chair, "It's okay Scrappy. You be good now and quiet down." The dog began to whine and cry, but after another minute, she was quiet."

"Another thing, you old Snake," the head biker continued, "you make any wrong moves, you or that dead man in the bed, and I'll feed both of you to the fishes. Which reminds me," he turned to his gaunt companion, "Billy, check out how sick the guy in the bed is."

Billy, holding his hand to his mouth to muffle his uncontrollable chuckle, complied. "Sure thing, Vince. If he ain't sick, I'll make sure he is," he giggled on.

Standing over the prone body of Zak, Billy pulled back all the covers and grabbed him by the throat. "If this guy with the chopped-up mug ain't dead, he's close to it Vinny."

"Whatever, keep an eye on him," Vince ordered.

Sam watched contemptuously as Vince rambled on. "Reno, look around, maybe outside. There must be some rope someplace in this joint." Then he turned to Sam. "Sorry, Sam the man, but we're going to have to tie up

CHAPTER 3

those meat hook hands of yours real good. I don't like your snotty attitude, old codger. Might be we'll have to rough you up a bit so we can convince you to share in the gold. If that's the way you want it, we'll oblige."

As Reno opened the locked door, the dog became aroused again and began to growl and bark.

Sam called out, "It's okay Scrappy, you be a good girl and lay down." The dog did as she was told, but her eyes followed the man menacingly as he crossed the yard.

"I'm going to tell you something, Vinny, or whatever your name is," Sam staunchly pronounced. "There is no gold, never has been, and for forty years I've told a thousand people the same thing. You're whistling Dixie pal, just like everyone before you. You want something to eat, take what you want from the icebox."

Vince smiled broadly through discolored teeth as he walked to the small table, placing his hands at each corner. "No gold, huh? Well, ain't that just about the biggest gosh darn lie in the Sierra Mountains. There's gold, old man, and if we have to, we're going to get it out of the only vein we have up here—yours." Reno returned from outside the cabin carrying a circle of heavy rope.

Vince grumbled, "Reno, tie this old bastard to the chair. We got some coaxing to do." Billy chuckled louder than usual. Tied tightly to the chair, Sam sat stoically, his defiant eyes staring straight forward.

Vince dropped to his knees directly in front of Sam. "Sam, I'm going to give you one more chance to save yourself from the ravages of 'Billy the Kid' here."

Unexpectedly, Vince turned to look again at the ghostly form of Zak stretched out in the big wooden bed. "Wait a minute, Billy boy, I'm sorry to disappoint you, but I got a better way to change old Sam's attitude. How about the big ailing stiff in the bed?" Vince straightened up and began to walk toward the reclined, innate figure.

"Yeah, that's it," he continued, "I think Sam might not like seeing the one he's cared for so much suffer even more. Would you, Sam?" Standing directly over the disfigured face of the silent Zak, Vince placed a pillow over the helpless victim. "In his condition, Sam, this shouldn't take long—unless, of course, we hear some magic words from you."

"Okay, okay," came immediate, desperate words from Sam. "You win, Vince. Yes, I have gold, and plenty of it, maybe millions. I'll bargain with you for this man's life, but only on my terms."

"Now, ain't that a lot easier, Sam? Imagine what might have happened," Vince quipped. "And besides, Sammy boy, this way both you and your scar-faced pal live to enjoy a long and prosperous partnership. We're not greedy; we'll leave ten percent of the gold with you two, just to prove my heart is in the right place."

"It's in the mine, the gold," Sam spoke quietly. "It's back in one of the deep chambers, in a tunnel only I can find. Without me, no one finds it or ever gets back. My bargain is simple, Vinny; first, I go nowhere with my hands tied, especially in that treacherous mine. Secondly, I want you all to swear on the Holy Bible in that drawer that no harm will come to the guy in the bed, whose name I don't even know. That's it; either do this my way or kill both of us and you get zero."

"Sam, Sam, that you should have such a rotten opinion of me and my God-fearing friends," Vince smiled. "A bargain is a bargain, Sam. Bring out the good book and Reno will cut the rope, Billy will get on his knees and pray, and the Lord will show us the way."

Ambling across the room, Reno displayed a switchblade knife with which he swiftly cut Sam's ropes.

Rubbing his reddened wrists, Sam explained their position. "We will wait until morning—now ain't the time to go mining."

"We will go now old man, we like to keep on the move," came Vince's rebuff.

THE INTRUDERS

Sam shook his head in disgust before giving them instructions: "Your friend Reno knows where the rope is, have him bring plenty. There are two special flashlights in the chest, bring those. I only have one helmet light, which I'll wear, and I'll carry a few hooks and pulleys." He paused, "Let me take one final look at my injured guest, and if you're determined, we'll start immediately.

Vince nodded as Sam walked over to Zak's side. Taking his hand to check for a pulse, he whispered. "Take care old pal, whoever you are. I'll be back in a few hours to check on you again." Undetected by his captives, Sam's mouth dropped as he saw Zak slightly raise his eyelids, communicating an awareness of events.

Sam turned quickly. "Ok, let's hit it and we can be back in maybe three or four hours."

Vince walked over to the bed, looking cautiously at the lifeless stranger, and motioned to Reno. "Only two of us go; Reno, you stay here in case this big dead heap comes to life. Any trouble at all, you know what to do. That's part of my bargain, Sam, whether you like it or not."

Momentarily, Sam hesitated, then responded, "Let's get with it, I don't want to spend any more time with you than I have to." He, Vince, and the smirking Billy left the cabin, carrying the load of mining implements.

CHAPTER 4
CATASTROPHE

Flickering light rays and huge, eerie shadows blanketed the claustrophobic walls of the long-abandoned mineshaft. Sam's helmet light beaconed the way through a constant mist of dusty air. The awkward figures of Vince and Billy stumbled forward, obviously having difficulty in negotiating the jagged terrain.

"Hey old timer," shouted Vince, "not so fast with the feet, pal, these motorcycle boots ain't exactly made for this kind of work."

Sam halted, "We'll be using ropes and pulleys soon, Mr. Vince, so you had better get those boots ready for the real test. Not to mention that my lung disease and this dust might leave you with no guide at all."

Grabbing Sam by the collar and pushing his revolver to his face, Vince growled, "No tricks, Pop, or you die right here and now in this hellhole."

In the semi-dark cabin, Reno stood looking out the small unclear window. The old man's dog, now tied to a tree, kept her keen eyes focused on the cabin. A ground fog began to envelop the blackened forest outside. Unable to vocalize, Reno's eyes uncommonly served as his source of expression. His giant frame belied an inner fear of the overwhelming silence associated with the high mountain country.

Fingering the heavy wooden window shutters, Reno's thick, unruly hair tangled over heavy eyebrows, and his unblinking eyes stared at the forest night in hypnotic uneasiness.

A haunting groan sound from the dark form in the bed brought Reno's bulky frame whirling around in such force that he slammed into the log wall. Momentarily frozen, he pulled himself away to cautiously approach the inanimate figure.

Towering over the unconscious stranger, Reno's black eyes widened in panic. He pulled the rag-doll figure to a sitting position. In desperation, he began to shake the limp body as though demanding another sound of life.

Suddenly, an unearthly crackling sound echoed though the small room as Zak's hand, glowing with a strange, other-worldly light and without warning, powerfully clamped onto Reno's neck. Breathing his last, Reno made a hideous guttural noise— his first sound in twenty-six years.

CHAPTER 4

Reno's body twisted, then stiffened and toppled in a loud thud to the cabin floor. An odor of burnt flesh emanated from his huge frame and then disappeared amidst a waving circle of smoke.

Puffing laboriously deep within the mine labyrinth, Vince yelled, "Ok, gold digger, I'm only going to tell you one more time, hold up, slow down now!" Charging up and into Sam's back, Vince jammed his gun under Sam's helmet. "I know what you're trying to pull, smart guy, so if I have to stop you one more time in this dungeon, I'll bury you here."

Sam, his face masked in heavy dust, smiled coolly. "Vince, like most idiots, you've run out your string. Go ahead, tough guy, shoot your gun off real loud, and we'll all get crushed in the cave in. Or maybe you and your laughing hyena friend Billy, who seems to be far behind us, would like to push me into one of the deep pits. That way, the two of you would have to find your own way back. Hell, you could use Billy's giggling as some kind of sonar detector. I'd guess in two or three months, one of you might find your way out, but I doubt it."

Terror filled the eyes of the usually brash Vince. He looked back into the shadowy dark tunnel where his gangly, coughing partner Billy struggled to keep up. A flapping of bats rambled across their heads like an eerie, suffocating blanket.

"These lights—how long can they last?" Vince's voice cracked.

"Beats me," came a caustic reply from Sam.

"Billy!" Vince screamed, "What the hell is the matter with you? Why are you always so far behind? Get your ass up here, fast!" Sam just stood watching his two stumblebums stagger in futility. "We got to rest," exclaimed Vince, his body crumbling to a sitting position against the dampened wall.

"Rest and you die in this place," retorted Sam, "which is what my emphysema is gonna do to me anyway."

"You win, old man," Vince fearfully accepted. "Just get us the hell out of here, Sam, and I swear we'll just leave as quickly as we came."

Billy dropped to his knees, billows of dust particles surrounding him. "Sam, I think I'm dying from lung disease too in this filthy air. Forget the gold, man. Just show us the way out, help me breathe—I'll do anything you want; I swear."

"What happened to our laughing boy Billy?" Sam quipped. "Too late to turn back now, my wayfaring friends, the gold is just around the corner. Follow me now or die where you are, but I'm going on."

CHAPTER 4

Sam's helmet light focused on the narrow tunnel ahead as a blur of dust particles filled its opening. Vince and Billy scrambled to their feet, stumbling in a panic to follow their lifeline, Sam Rooney.

Now fully awake, Zak turned slowly to his side, and a few bed covers fell to the floor.

My God, what happened? Zak questioned. *My arm seems to be vibrating like I have a seizure. And the big guy, all I did was grab him by the neck. What the heck's going on? I don't get it.* Sitting himself up on his elbows, Zak surveyed the cabin. *Wonder how long I've been here, and Sam—I've got to find out what happened to him.*

Looking down at his left hand and stretching his fingers, Zak spoke aloud. "It's gloomy in here and I'm not focusing too well, but I swear my hand has a weird glow to it." Remembering that Sam had cleverly placed a piece of paper in his hand when he had last approached the bed, Zak opened his fist and a small note curled from his palm. Unfolding the note, Zak carefully read its contents.

"I wrote this note as a safeguard while mining this vein for over thirty years. Many interested characters have attempted to find out if the rumors of my gold

strike were true. Until now, I've been successful in warding off all intrusions. By the time you read this note, chances are I'm dead, and whoever my adversaries are, they're dead too. Believe me, it would take more than one to overtake me. Having given you—whoever you are—this note, I've handed you the treasure of my life savings and the responsibilities that go along with it. I have always prayed that if a life and death situation came, the Lord would send me a messenger; I pray you're it. A map on the back of this note details the directions to my life's work. It belongs to my only daughter, Lisa Tamara, and her husband Andrew. They know nothing of this, or of my whereabouts. Last time I heard, they lived in a small town called Wayzata, in Minnesota. Tell her of my love and that I am sorry for my strange, reclusive ways. God speed, stranger, and may you do that to allow me to rest in peace. Thanks, Sam Rooney."

Zak stuffed the note into his pocket. Painfully, he eased himself from the bed and stepped over the massive carcass of Reno. As he passed the small, dirty window, he caught a glimpse of his now scarred, unrecognizable face. He allowed himself no time to absorb the shock.

CHAPTER 4

Attempting to move quickly, he opened the cabin door and staggered down the narrow path leading to the mine.

Nearing the entrance, a muffled explosion could be heard. The ground around him shuddered and a shower of smoke, gas, and debris belched from the mine opening. Falling to his knees, Zak knew it was dynamite, and it was likely hidden and ignited by Sam. A thunder of cave-ins followed in sequence. Within minutes, the mine and its entryway were filled with the mountain's internal rubble.

Lying on his stomach, Zak could feel another series of tremors reverberating underground. Unsteadily rising to his feet, he spoke again aloud, "Sam, one thing I can promise, you will rest in peace.

CATASTROPHE

CHAPTER 5
A JOURNEY BEGINS

Struggling back to the cabin, Zak saw the old dog that had helped save his life tied to a tree. Zak went over to the dog and patted her on the head and untied her. Immediately, the dog ran toward the old mine entrance in search of her master. Back inside, Zak took the gun from Reno's body and hurriedly rummaged through an old supply chest. He would need supplies to travel the heavy woods and cross any designated rivers or streams on Sam's map. Finding a backpack, a blanket roll, some canned goods, and a smattering of hiking tools, Zak wasted little time in making his way outside and down a path leading to the water's edge. He vaguely remembered someone talking about an old boat that Sam kept nearby. The first rays of morning sun revealed the boat only a few yards from where the path ended.

Throwing his pack into the boat, Zak stepped into an old plat-bottom relic when he heard a noise. Loping down the dark, narrow path came Mule; the sturdy donkey Sam had tenderly cared for. Looking dolefully at Zak, the muscular little animal sounded a few he-haws.

A JOURNEY BEGINS

"Wish I could take you, partner, but there just isn't any room and the water moves a lot faster than you." With a great effort he shoved off into the swift current, watching Mule drink from the cool water.

Using one of the old ores as a rudder, Zak knelt in the boat, maneuvering the waterway and its scattering of rocks. He had read the first part of Sam's map and felt the river would best take him to the first leg of the unknown journey.

Shortly into the river excursion, Zak caught a glimpse of a flash of light from the forest. Although the morning had come, the light—or its reflection—beamed brightly.

I should probably go on, he thought, *but my instincts or curiosity won't let me.*

With surprising skill, he guided the cumbersome boat to the river's edge. Remembering the gun he had taken from Reno, Zak placed it inside a small pack he wore. Pulling the boat a few feet up on the shore, he proceeded toward the bright light. He saw it again, two or three times, through the maze of trees while he cautiously continued in the direction of the source.

Using the concealment of the underbrush, Zak came upon the object of his search; three dirt-crusted Harley-Davidsons motorcycles. On one of them, a rearview mirror faced directly into the sun, reflecting a burning brilliance.

"Must have belonged to the three weirdos," Zak surmised. "They got as far as they could by bike and walked through the woods to Sam's cabin. I wonder; if they made it this far, there must be a trail or path close by. That path could lead to a road, maybe even the main highway like the one shown on Sam's map."

Surveying his surroundings, Zak found an old Indian path where the obscure tracks of the motorcycles were still apparent. After checking the saddlebags of each cycle and finding nothing but stale cans of beer, spoiled sausages, and some dirty magazines, Zak crossed an ignition wire to start the bike containing the most gasoline.

The classic roar of a Harley-Davidson motor in the wild high-country brought many birds to flight. As Zak looked up through the trees, a sense of surrealism filled his mind.

"Crazy," he said, "here I sit in the middle of the wilderness on a motorcycle, expecting to follow a faded map to who knows where. Sam, whoever you were and whatever drove you to prepare this map, I'm compelled to complete your wishes."

Dumping the remaining bikes into the river and sinking the old boat, Zak mounted the Harley to fishtail down the unknown mud trail and headed due east, as the map dictated. He wore Sam's blue hooded sweatshirt he had stuffed into the backpack, as it helped conceal his disfigured face. The powerful motorcycle churned forward, a white smoke trailing from the rumbling exhaust, giving Zak a good feeling.

Occasionally stopping to verify certain landmarks designated on the rough map, Zak calculated that a highway should appear soon. To his delight, and earlier than expected, the path ended at a mountain black-top road. From there, a short distance further, California State Highway 166 verified the map's accuracy.

Now accelerating at a high rate of speed, a feeling of elation spread throughout Zak's body. He was on course, the map proved correct, and even his strength and appetite were improving.

A dissolute landscape surrounded his field of vision. Bare of any populated homes or traffic, the motorcycle's growl echoed throughout the void. Then, over a gradual rise, a small diner came unexpectedly into view.

One car was parked in front of the diner, and it was close to the entrance door. Zak pulled the bike alongside the lone car and slowly entered the small café. A customer sat at the far end of the counter talking quietly to the waitress. They both turned to observe Zak as he sat at a stool close to the register.

"Welcome to Hannah's Place, stranger," the pert little waitress announced while strutting in Zak's direction, her curvaceous figure swaying sensually. "Coffee, tea, or me, as they say in the sky, so why not coffee and pie, I always say. Right mister? Just kidding."

A smile crossed Zak's face and he looked slightly downward.

"The shy type," she continued through pronounced gum chewing, "or are you auditioning for the lead in *Phantom of the Opera*?"

Zak's smiled broadened, and he replied, "If the script calls for gulping down two cheeseburgers in record time, I'll take the part."

Hannah laughed and called the cheeseburger order to her cook, standing behind a horizontal opening in the wall.

Turning back to her newly arrived customer, Hannah quipped, "And to drink, Mr. Phantom, how about a beer?"

"Sounds good to me, sweetheart, and make it cold, if that's possible for you," he chided.

Looking over Zak's shoulder and out the diner window, Hannah recognized a familiar car. "Well, if it ain't the official freeloaders with badges."

Zak turned on his stool to see a California State Police car parked next to his stolen motorcycle. Slowly, he turned back to the counter and casually commented, "Hannah, you'd better run, maybe they're looking to arrest someone for disorderly conduct."

She laughed again. "If that's the case, I'm happy to say I'm guilty." Even Zak laughed.

"Howdy, Gypsy," one of the two police officers said upon entering.

Hannah acknowledged, "Howdy boys. Take your usual front row seats." The smiling officers proceeded to the far end of the counter.

"What's with 'Gypsy', Hannah?" Zak queried.

"I used to be an exotic dancer," she replied, "and the best too; they called me Hard Hearted Hannah."

Hannah attended to the police officers, adding her usual tomfoolery. Zak managed an easy, natural demeanor when the officer sitting closest to him looked his way.

"Hey mister, excuse me, but is that your Harley-Davidson out there?"

Zak felt warmth rise in his neck, then half-turned and smiled, "Sure is."

The policeman got up from his stool and looked at Hannah. "Just coffee, Hannah. I'll be back in a minute, Clay," he said to his partner.

The officer proceeded to sit down next to Zak and continued his conversation. "Yeah, I couldn't help noticing that beautiful green bike, mister. I'm sure you know it's one-of-a-kind, and I've got to tell you, I ain't never seen that model in a dark green color. Kind of rare, isn't it?"

Zak turned fully; his face still shadowed by his hood. "Guess it is, I'm just partial to green."

"I got ya," the officer agreed. "I'm only bothering you because I have the same model in my garage at home. Mine's red, and I sure have a romance with that hog."

"No bother at all, officer, I understand," Zak responded.

The officer stood up. "Maybe I'll see you around again cruising the highway and we can talk Harleys." He paused. "One thing I would like to ask you—any reason why you don't have license plates?"

"I just bought the bike yesterday and plan to pick up the plates tomorrow," Zak answered.

"Well, any man who drives the same bike as I do can't be all bad, I reckon."

At that moment, the other police officer walked up carrying two cups of coffee. "No time for jawing, Troy, we'll take our coffee to go," he urged. "Headquarters reports an eighteen-wheeler has gone over the ridge at Cheyenne Point."

Officer Troy Williams headed for the door, his partner following behind. Just before exiting, the officer made a parting comment to Zak. "Get those license plates real quick, will you pal? I wouldn't want to ticket a fellow Harley brother."

Hannah poured Zak a cup of coffee. "As far as I'm concerned, I just saved my restaurant two free breakfasts," she exclaimed. "As for you, Mr. Phantom, I'll have your cheeseburgers in a jiffy. In case you would like to read a newspaper, be my guest," she said, handing him the morning paper.

Scanning the small local newspaper, Zak saw that most of the news told of the various towns struggling to recover from the recent monstrous storm. However, a small two-inch column reported a sketchy account of a body found in an old mining cabin, high in the Sierra Madres. Zak took a double take when he read that the body found was that of a drifter, who according to the article, died from being struck by lightning.

"By lightning," he blurted out. "How the heck did they surmise that?" he mused.

Finishing his meal, Zak walked to the cashier counter as Hannah also approached. She pulled a pencil from behind her ear, popped a bubble of gum, and caustically spoke. "That'll be six dollars even, Phantom. Tell me, if you don't mind, is there any special reason why you wear that hood so low? No one can see your beautiful face!"

Zak paid the amount of money requested and replied, "Who knows, Hannah, maybe I'm a temperamental movie star and just want to be left alone." He turned to walk toward the exit door.

Hannah tiptoed quickly from behind the register and came up behind him. "I just gotta know, mister!" She yelled, and yanked Zak's hood from his face. Her eyes widened and her body repelled against the cashier case. "Oh mister, I'm sorry, I didn't know. I thought you were fooling me, I'm...I'm..."

Zak pulled the hood back, opened the door, and retorted, "Now we both know why they call you Hard Hearted Hannah, right?" He walked out.

A JOURNEY BEGINS

Sam Rooney's raw, but accurate map called for a continuation on Route 166 to Interstate Highway 99 and on into the Greenhorn Mountains of the Sierra Nevada. Zak pondered how Sam did more traveling than most people realized. He also remembered how Sam never disturbed any of Zak's personal belongings, including his small wallet containing documents and money.

The grumbling Harley-Davidson carried him on through the foothills between the Sierra Madres and the scenic Greenhorn Mountain country. The day grew warmer and as nighttime neared, Zak thought of the possible difficulties in finding suitable lodging.

Rounding a sharp curve in the darkening highway, Zak spotted a small, partially secluded motel a few hundred yards off the main road. A bright neon sign flashed "The Red Rock Motel" and beneath that, *vacancies*, prompting him to pull into the adjacent parking lot. Surveying the neatly kept premises—with a limousine parked in front of a motel unit—he proceeded to the front office.

Without difficulty, Zak secured a double-bed unit. Turning the key to his room, a shuffling noise came from outside the room where the limousine was parked. He walked partway into his room before turning to watch.

CHAPTER 5

Two well-dressed men and a blond woman were arguing. The men appeared to be unable to convince the young lady to go with them into the limo.

The conversations became more intense, allowing Zak to hear the woman say, "I'm not going to that house ever again. No, no, there is no way you can convince me to come with you. Never."

One of the men shouted, "Teresa, you must come with us. Don't make me carry you out of here." She pulled herself away and proceeded toward the motel room when both men ran to apprehend her.

"Excuse me, gentlemen," came the effective voice of Zak as he suddenly loomed before the threesome. "Seems to me the lady has expressed opposition to your proposal, if I read her right."

All three froze from the unexpected encounter. "This is a family skirmish, mister, so don't butt in," demanded the taller man.

Zak slowly walked over to the woman. "If she tells me so, I'll apologize and go my way."

Both men looked at the now disheveled woman as she pulled herself from their grasp and said defiantly, "I have asked them to leave, and that's what I want now."

Again, the tall one spoke, "Come on, Ron," motioning to his partner, "we can't reason with her now."

The two men entered the limousine. The man called Ron poked his head out the car window and shouted, "You're making a big mistake, mister. We'll be back." Leaving a long exhaust trail, the big car sped out of the parking lot and onto the main highway.

"Guess I owe you thanks, sir," the frail lady remarked.

Zak replied, "Well, it's none of my business, but is it really a family thing I broke up?"

She turned to lean on a small lattice railing, her long blonde hair hanging unruly. "Yes, my family, my family, it's always my family. Oh, how did this happen...I'm so sorry to involve you, an innocent bystander. Please, go back to your room or wherever you came from; I'll be fine. Just go and accept my thanks; maybe they won't bother you."

She walked back to her room, shaking her head. At the doorway, she turned, "Oh, I hope they don't take anything out on you."

"They? Who are they?" Zak asked, "I thought you said they were family."

The young lady pleaded, "If you can leave now, sir, I mean drive out of here and keep driving, please do."

CHAPTER 5

Zak approached her. "I'm going to get some much-needed sleep, Miss. If something happens during the night, my room number and phone is 101."

She watched quizzically as her protector—whose face she could not see—ambled toward his room.

His eyes opened from a deep sleep. The room was pitch black throughout, and Zak wondered why he had suddenly awoken. There had been no noise, no sound or wind. All surroundings were profoundly quiet.

Lying on his back, his hand resting on his forehead, Zak became aware of a weird glow. Looking up, he saw his hand reflecting a pale greenish-blue light. He jumped from the bed and quickly turned the overhead light on.

"Yikes!" he shouted, "what the heck was that?" Looking intently at his left hand, he could see nothing unusual. There was no glow, but the bothersome arm vibration had returned. There hung a floor-length mirror next to the bathroom, so he stood in front of it, holding his arm out; nothing abnormal.

Reaching to the right of the mirror for the wall switch, he turned the lights off. As though entering a dream and looking into a deep tunnel, the mirror revealed a strange, astonishing greenish-blue light encompassing his left arm.

"This must be a nightmare. I'll wake up at any moment now and it'll all be over," pleaded Zak. He turned and threw himself upon the bed, burying his arm beneath the pillows.

"Wake up, Zak, wake up!" he screamed. Pulling the pillow slowly from his arm, he cautiously looked again. Whatever light he saw, if indeed he had, disappeared. He went back to the mirror and turned the light on and off many times, but the glow did not reappear. Maybe, he thought, it was an illumination caused by lack of sleep or some imaginary factor.

Collapsing back onto the bed, he fell into a troubled, exhausted sleep. His subconscious mind conjured up a whirling, psychedelic picture of circular, neon-lighted tornadoes. Floating through space, Zak's arm became imprisoned within these rotating electrical beams, forcibly carrying him to the outer limits of the universe.

A relentless piercing sound entered the inner sanctum of this intensive nightmare. His eyes opened, recognizing the ringing telephone only inches from his head.

Grappling with the phone, Zak managed to answer, "Yes, yes, who is it?"

The familiar voice of the woman he had encountered that night spoke, "I'm sorry, I don't know your name, but this is Teresa, the girl you helped last night. Are you okay?" she asked. "You sound troubled."

"No, I just woke up, and well, I'm a lousy morning person," Zak mumbled.

"It isn't morning," she said, "it's just past noon, meaning you slept a long time, mister..." she hesitated.

Zak noticed the pause. "Zak— my name is Zak. Is everything all right with you?" he asked.

"Yes, I'm ok for now, and I thought you might like to join me for lunch in the motel restaurant?"

Zak paused a little too long, then responded, "See you in fifteen minutes."

When Zak entered the small motel restaurant, Teresa waved at him from a neat, checker-clothed table.

Sitting down, he remarked, "Well, young lady, you look a lot more relaxed and in control than you did last night."

"Yes, I'm sorry about that Zak. Those men, I hesitate to admit, are my brothers. The problem *is* a family thing, but it's just too long and complicated to explain now. I can tell you that my family is obsessed with me and what I do or where I go. That's why I asked you to join me for lunch. My brothers, and especially my father, might make some cockamamy issue out of your intervention. Can you just take my word for it and not stay around these premises any longer? I mean, can't you just hop on your motorcycle and go a few thousand miles somewhere else?"

Zak's familiar smirk appeared, and he spoke decisively, "Could I have some breakfast first, and maybe buy yours, and then you can explain some of the reasons why you're so anxious to get rid of me."

Teresa closed her eyes and shook her head. "Ok, Zak, but only if you promise to leave as soon as we finish our talk."

"It's a deal," he replied. "Now, I could really go for some scrambled eggs and burnt bacon."

A young waiter took their order and poured two steaming cups of coffee. Teresa raised her cup to drink it. "I guess you could say I'm sort of a maverick in my family," she said, "and let me just add, without a lengthy explanation, that my father is an important man in the glitzy town of Las Vegas. By that I mean he has a reputation of which some might consider unsavory if one believed all the publicity. He and I haven't seen or spoken to one another for years now; mostly because of my unapproved activities." She took a big gulp of the coffee and added, "Do you mind if I smoke?" Zak shook his head.

CHAPTER 5

During their breakfast, Teresa told a vague tale of a closely-knit family and her early rebellion from their traditions. She had left her wealthy lifestyle over four years ago, engaging in rebellious activities; all of which added fuel to her family's discontent.

"Sounds like a story I've heard a hundred times before, Teresa," Zak interrupted.

"Yes, I suppose so, but..." she looked down, "now I'm pregnant, and the father of my baby is missing, and..."

The door of the restaurant was thrown open by the force of her two brothers. One shouted, "Teresa, we've come back to take you home now! Don't make this morning one we'll all regret."

They both walked quickly over to Teresa and Zak. The older brother directed his attention to Zak. "Mister, do yourself a favor; stay seated, say nothing, and don't interfere in any way. This is a family problem, and we can handle it on our own time, you got it?" Zak remained silent.

Teresa jumped to her feet. "This guy is a perfect stranger. Morrow. You and Ronnie have no right to tell me what to do. What is it with you guys; are you crazy? You have no respect for me as a woman who wants to live her own life."

"I'm Morrow, mister," he said, motioning to Zak. "I'm asking you to maybe take a seat at the end booth over there or go for a walk. We just want a moment to talk to our sister privately; about our family and stuff, ok?"

Without a word, Zak stood up, looked grimly at both brothers, glanced at Teresa, and walked slowly to sit in a distant booth.'

Teresa's younger brother Ronnie leaned against a nearby wooden pillar, as though on guard, while Morrow spoke intently to her. "Teresa, Papa has asked that we do everything we can to plead with you to come back home and talk to him. He has promised not to insist on anything; not to demand, but to offer assistance. The old man is in pain over your running away and refuses to say anything. He knows about the baby. Teresa, he's our father. At least give him the time to speak his piece; you owe him that. Besides, he's been in a lot of pain recently, and has been in and out of the hospital with his crippled condition."

"Morrow, I love Papa, but the many times we've talked before ended up in terrible arguments, getting nowhere," Teresa replied sadly.

Morrow leaned over, taking her hand. "Teresa, that was long ago, before Papa lost Mama. Time has taken its toll, believe me. He's reached a calm in his life and needs your consolation. To prove my point, Teresa, your Papa came with us today; he's in the car outside. When have you known him to leave the upstairs office for anyone?

"Papa's here, in the car, outside this motel?" exclaimed Teresa. "He must be ill or it's another one of his skillful maneuvers." She threw her head back, "Ok, ok, but I'm not going to the car. Tell Papa to come here, into the restaurant, and we can talk."

Coincidentally, at that moment, a noisy rustling occurred at the restaurant entrance door. A tall man dressed in a chauffeur's uniform attempted to open the double doors to the main entrance. Kicking the normally unused door open, the chauffeur helped manipulate a heavy, electronically controlled wheelchair, supporting a well-dressed heavy-set man, through the opening.

"Papa, Papa!" Teresa screamed as she ran to the handicapped figure, embracing him warmly. The moment revealed a special feeling shared by a father and daughter.

"My little girl," he spoke softly, his dark bluish-black eyes misty beneath heavy grey eyebrows. "Your Papa has missed you dearly, and I have been wrong not coming to see you sooner. The time has come for you and me to remember our family, especially your departed mother, and what she would want."

"I know, Papa. I know how painful our relationship has been for almost two years now," Teresa responded tearfully.

"Come, Papa," Teresa continued, "steer your chair to our table, we have many things to talk about and to settle."

Her father, managing a slight smile, pulled a partially fallen blanket to his shrunken knees and reached for her hand. He then pushed the control buttons on the mechanical wheelchair, maneuvering himself into position at the small table where his sons Ronnie and Morrow stood. "Everybody, please sit down," their father asked, "we are together again. Your dear Mother would be so happy."

Among a gathering of smiles and tender expressions, a cajoling family shared their warm moment. Teresa's father waved his arm, directing the waiter, "Sir, it's never too early for wine; please bring me a carafe of your finest red. My sons and daughter have joined with me again in salutations."

He then turned sharply in his chair to look in the direction of Zak, sitting in the distant booth. "And you, the one with the buried face who I believe has an acquaintance with my daughter, come join us. Maybe you can add some insight into my Teresa's present life."

Surprised, Zak rose and slowly walked toward the four family members, extending his hand. "My name is Zak, and I appreciate your asking me to join you, but I have only just met your lovely daughter."

Teresa's father smiled and shook Zak's hand. "Well, if you've known her at all, come and share our wine and perhaps offer whatever you can. These are my sons, Ronnie and Morrow, and my name is Philip Maniatis. Mr. Zak, pull up a chair and consider yourself welcome."

Tentatively, Zak pulled a nearby chair to the table. He had heard the name Philip Maniatis before and realized his host represented the hierarchy of the Las Vegas gambling empire.

Pouring a round for everyone, Maniatis raised his glass and proceeded through holding court. "To my sons, our guest, and especially to my daughter who has returned to the family."

"Opa!" yelled Ronnie, wincing slightly from the wine.

Making a sharp gesture, Mr. Maniatis continued. "Teresa, it has been a long time, too long, and your brothers and I want your happiness more than anything. Our home is yours, and yes, the new baby's as well. In fact, we have remodeled a few rooms to accommodate both of your needs. It is with love and respect that we hope you come home now, today."

Turning in obvious pain from his misfunctioning legs, her father's eyes held steadily upon Teresa, his voice concise. "No rules or restrictions, as I realize that perhaps I've been overly protective in the past. As for your motorcycle companion here, allow me some patience to understand this relationship you have."

Teresa placed her hands on the table. "Papa, my motorcycle companion is, as I have told you, a passing acquaintance whom I have just met. Why do you always interpret my relationships with men as a front to you and my family loyalty? You want me to come home, and you speak of loyalty and trust, but then you infer a relationship between this stranger and myself. Papa, this man Zak befriended me yesterday, and that's all there is to it."

She pulled back her long hair. "Only you would comment on his motorcycle, and probably a few other things have already been checked out." With a deep breath, Teresa continued, "If you really mean what you say, I ask that you start by letting this innocent bystander leave now. Let him take his bike and drive away freely."

"Teresa, you misunderstand my intentions, my purpose," Philip Maniatis insisted. "Your friend Zak is a guest at our table, and as such, commands our respect to do whatever he pleases. Mr. Zak," he whirled his electric wheelchair around, "if I have offended you, as a concerned father, please accept my apology and any assistance I can offer you. I would like to add, however, I believe this is the first meeting I've had with a man whose face I haven't seen. That hood you wear, sir—and I apologize again—can be distracting and misleading."

A strained silence fell upon the group as Zak slowly rose to his feet. "Gentlemen, Teresa, thanks for the wine, but I'll be on my way."

Quickly, Teresa replied, "Zak, I'll be alright now, and I do wish you a safe journey with a strong wind at your back."

Zak walked to the door, turning as he opened it, "Teresa, I hope you and your family find the kind of peace a trusting family is all about. In the meantime, Mr. Maniatis, I'll probably contact you sometime in the future to inquire about your daughter's welfare, if you don't mind. See you later." With a final nod, he left.

"Well, Papa," Teresa sighed, "I guess it's time to go home now. I'll need a few minutes to pack my clothes, so I'll meet you back here in twenty minutes." She stood up and quickly scampered from the restaurant. Her father maneuvered his electric wheelchair toward the entrance.

He opened the restaurant door and peered outside. With a slight hand gesture, he motioned to his sons.

Morrow and Ronnie approached their father, and Ronnie spoke. "Yes, Papa, what is it you want?"

Philip Maniatis bowed his head and pressed his temples tightly between his large hands. "The strange guy on that obnoxious motorcycle, I think he's heading toward Bakersfield, and I have certain doubts about him. There is no time to check him out thoroughly, so see that he doesn't make it there."

Maniatis whirled the wheelchair back to their table to finish his wine and give further instructions. "Morrow, Ronnie, make your own arrangements for transportation; your sister and I are going home. He leaned back, glancing at the chauffeur, "Frank, check that my daughter is getting ready and assist her in carrying her bags."

CHAPTER 6
THE CONFRONTATION

A growing warmth from the morning desert sun felt good on the tired face of Zak. It was a rare moment where his heavy, cotton hood lay pinned against his back from the strong wind manufactured by the moving Harley-Davidson. The road ahead swallowed up quickly beneath the churning wheels of the glistening metal steed. A thin smile creased his exposed, scarred face, and an unexpected ease calmed his edgy nature. A small highway sign reading *Pine Flat* flashed by, almost unnoticed, as Zak turned his head in recognition of the nearing small town.

Pine Flat, California proved to be just that; a small, arid oasis surrounded by a few pine trees. But his weary body, along with the troublesome circumstances back at the Red Rock Motel, plagued his inner self. Slowing his pace, Zak sashayed the dusty motorcycle into a seemingly deserted gas station. Seeing no one, he dismounted. Taking the hose from the gas pump, he proceeded to pour gas into the almost empty tank.

THE CONFRONTATION

After filling the gas tank and checking other mechanical functions, Zak walked to the gas station office. Opening a sticky door, he encountered an old, white-bearded man sleeping soundly at an antique desk.

"Excuse me, mister, I just pumped seven dollars' worth of gas. Can somebody give me change for a ten-dollar bill?"

The old man looked over steel-rimmed glasses and spoke in rapid fire fashion. "Saw you coming in all the way, son. Ain't no need to help them that can help themselves, I always say. The register is right in back of me, so drop in your ten and take three out, and I appreciate the business." Sure enough, the cash register was behind him with the drawer open.

"Whatever you say, sir," Zak replied. "It's been a long time since I've seen the honor system used in any business."

"Been robbed eight times, son, but it ain't enough to close me down or change my sleeping habits," the old man retorted.

"Whatever makes you feel good, mister," answered Zak, "in the meantime, I wonder if you know of a place I can get a room for the night; I could use a day's rest."

CHAPTER 6

"No problem, stranger, on this side of the street and only a block down. The name is Shady Rest; not the best, but it'll pass the test. Tell them Sid sent you."

Zak thanked the man and started to leave, when suddenly and without warning, the aching vibration he experienced in his arm the previous night rippled through his fingers.

"Is there a restroom inside here?" Zak asked.

"Huh, sure." the old man replied, "You have to go outside to the side of the building that way." He said, pointing in the direction. "Are you ok? What is it with your arm, stranger?"

Zak staggered against the small counter. "I'm okay, Sid. Just a Charlie horse." He quickly opened the station door and ran around to the outside.

Zak reached for the door marked "restroom" with his unaffected hand, only to discover that it was locked. Instinctively, he switched to the tremoring left hand, and the lock easily snapped open.

"My God, I broke the lock effortlessly." Scrambling inside the dark and cramped washroom quarters, he flicked the light switch, but it didn't work. Suddenly, the strange bluish glow appeared again, creating enough light in the dark room to allow him to see himself. The mirror over the small sink reflected a scary green and blue silhouette.

There was no doubt that his left arm resembled a glowing neon light. Putting his arm up to the mirror to examine it closer, Zak's mind raced in confusion. "What are you? Where did you come from, and what's this all about?" There appeared to be a mild tremor creating an almost indistinguishable array of sparks that resembled a short circuit.

Holding his arm flush to the mirror, his eyes inches away, Zak took a deep breath and spoke aloud. "Whatever this glow is, the pain has diminished, and I feel an enormous power in my hand. It had to be the result of those high-tension wires and the storm; crazy." He reacted in a jolt to what sounded like a car backfiring. Then, it happened again, and he knew they were gunshots.

Zak raced from the restroom. "Sid, Sid," he yelled, and as he rounded the building, a small man wearing a black ski mask aimed a gun at him and fired; but it misfired. In panic and self-defense, Zak swung a fist at the dark figure, ripping the ski mask from his face. An electro-static sound emerged, and the dark figure screamed in agony, electrified. His body crumpled in a heap to the ground, withering in a snake-like curl. Zak stood dazed and astounded by what had just happened. He realized he had hit this figure with his glowing, vibrating arm.

The sound of a car door opening drew his attention. Another ski-masked individual stepped from a pick-up truck parked alongside the two gasoline pumps. The figure took one step toward Zak, saw his partner lying on the ground, then turned and jumped back into the truck, speeding away.

Zak ran after the vehicle, just managing to grab the rear tailgate with his glowing hand, "Hold it, fella, hold it!" he shouted. But the truck soon disappeared in a cloud of dust, down and through the main part of town.

Standing in the gas station parking lot and breathing heavily, Zak slowly looked down at his now partially glaring hand holding the tailgate of the truck. He had unknowingly ripped it from its mounting. "Holy cow, this thing is scarier than I thought."

Running back to the station office, Zak could see the bearded man Sid laying across the desk with two bullet holes in his head. Shocked and frightened, but unable to help the man, he grabbed the phone, dialed the operator, and told her to send the police. After a few moments, he was able to get some semblance of his composure back and he walked to his motorcycle, cranked the machine once, and it burst to a start. With a growl, the bike lurched forward, and he wheeled himself out of Pine Flat.

Darkness fell on the desolate expanse of the open highway. Only the bright single headlight beam of the fast-moving motorcycle pierced the blackness.

I'm tired, but I've got a full tank of gas, and I could cover a lot of ground, Zak pondered. *Whatever, I'm on a northeasterly course, as Sam's map dictates, and I'd better put some distance between Pine Flat and myself.* The bike's small, red taillight faded swiftly into the night.

As the night drew on, the drone of the bike engine brought frequent nodding, so Zak decided to pull off the road. He hoped to find a cover of brush or trees and possibly put together a makeshift sleeping bag. The bike wheels sunk slightly into the sand, and the scattering of sagebrush forced a zigzagging motion while Zak searched for an isolated spot. Reaching the base of a rock formation, he decided to pull up. Quickly throwing whatever clothing he carried onto the ground, Zak collapsed into a deep sleep.

Awaking to the sound of a loud ticking noise made by a strange-looking bird, Zak realized he had enjoyed a long, uninterrupted rest despite the events of the previous day. The sun had already begun to warm the desert, and white sparkle from the dry sand emerged.

Maybe the strange glow and vibration will temper and fade away with time, he reflected, while examining the return to normalcy of his left arm.

He was surprised to see that the refuge he had found stood at the foothills of the majestic Sierra Nevada Mountains. Examining the frayed map again, Zak knew he still had a long journey through the mountains and onto the great Mojave Desert, and eventually a town called Stovepipe Wells in Death Valley.

Cruising the Sequoia National Forest and encircled by the grandeur of its beauty, Zak began to relax and enjoy the wonders of nature. His bike moved briskly, and the sky bristled blue through the openings of emerald foliage. A slight breeze brought a touch of sweet fragrance, prompting him to remove the dark cotton hood from his face once again. He leaned back on the bike and proceeded up the mountain's winding road with ease. A broad smile came gradually through the maze of his scarred face.

His reverie soon abated when a roadblock came into view. Orange and black wooden horses and flashing yellow lights manned by two forest rangers impeded his path.

THE CONFRONTATION

"Hold up, mister. We've got some big fire trouble up Maggie Mountain," a voice shouted.

Zak pulled his bike to a stop alongside the rangers. "Guess I must be one of the few who haven't heard of the fire, huh?" he asked.

One ranger—a sergeant—walked toward him. "You got it, sir; although we've been at this darn inferno for three days, we just now moved our barricades back to this point."

Zak now saw smoke in the distance and recognized the smell of burning trees. The ranger leaned on Zak's bike. "Ain't no way I can let you through, mister. Our rangers and firefighters got their hands full."

"I understand, Sergeant, but if you would allow me, I might be able to help. This motorcycle is easy to maneuver, and I've had a lot of experience as a lineman working through the high country. If you're short-handed, I'm willing to volunteer."

The sergeant turned to his partner. "Sounds good to me. How about it, Al?" His partner nodded in the affirmative. "Go ahead, mister." The sergeant relented, pulling away from the barricade. "But if it gets too hot for you, at least pull down that heavy hood you're wearing, will you?"

CHAPTER 6

Zak waved, and in a roar, the Harley carried him full tilt toward the thin white smoke. "Sure hope this thing ain't as bad as the monster of '92; I thought my time had come then," Zak murmured to himself. Within minutes, the small motorcycle disappeared into a heavy cloud of smoke.

It didn't take long for Zak to become embroiled in the activity of firefighters running about. Some shouted instructions as they jumped over hoses or ropes encompassing the road.

Someone wearing a white and gold helmet of authority called out to Zak. "Hey, you on the motorcycle, have you ever driven a bulldozer?"

Zak pulled the bike to the side of the fire chief. "Yes, I have, maybe a hundred yards or so."

"There's a newly plowed path to the right; take that as far as it goes," the firefighter commanded. "You'll find the bulldozer that piled through a trench until the driver was overcome by smoke. We have two other dozers on the job trying to dig other paths long enough to break the fire. We could sure use the third tractor, mister."

"Got ya," Zak responded, powering the bike over the heavy hoses lining the narrow road. The tracks of bulldozer work came quickly into view, and he stood up on the motorcycle to soften the blows from the rough, plowed path. Smoke became more intense, and he could feel intense heat coming from one side.

Like a medieval metal monster, the shadow of the abandoned bulldozer rose through the smoke ahead. Leaving the motorcycle alongside a tree, Zak wondered if he would ever see the prized bike again.

Leaping atop the silent steel Caterpillar, he immediately started the powerful diesel engine. Maneuvering the huge machine into position, he deftly continued in the proposed direction.

I would guess this angle leads to the closest road, Zak thought to himself. *If I could make it to that point, I'm sure it will help.*

An hour into the grueling project of downing trees, crushing rocks, and burrowing through an almost impenetrable terrain, Zak could finally see the distant highway. Smoke and heat, as well as a flickering of approaching flames, hastened his objective.

Only yards from the open road, Zak observed the cab of a semi-trailer truck on the highway lying on its side. He could see what appeared to be a man's leg protruding from under the cab.

Jumping from the bulldozer, Zak ran to the accident scene. To his fear, an unconscious form lay partly under the overturned truck cab.

CHAPTER 6

"Hey, fella, can you hear me?" he shouted. There came no response. Whatever had caused the accident, the driver had seemingly been thrown under the massive chassis.

Crawling atop the truck, Zak opened the partially crushed door in hopes of finding a portable phone or first aid kit; but neither was to be found. There were, however, some blankets and a coffee thermos, which he carried back to the unconscious man.

A trickle of blood flowed from under the body. "Oh no!" he exclaimed, "This guy is going to bleed to death. Maybe if I can use one of those heavy logs as a wedge, I can slide the cab enough to pull him out."

Zak hustled back to the area he had pulverized and returned carrying a large piece of a log. Placing the heavy timber underneath the front fender, he hopelessly attempted to create some small movement. Grunting and straining to the fullest, the situation appeared impossible.

Much to Zak's surprise, the victim slowly turned his head. Glassy eyes revealed a semi-conscious state as he spoke. "Friend, ain't no way you can help me with that. There is a portable phone somewhere under me; call 911 if you can." He slipped back into unconsciousness.

In a panic, Zak crawled beneath the truck's undercarriage and stretched his arm in a vain attempt to feel for the phone. Hang on fella, I'll find that phone if—" Then it happened. The blue-green glow from his arm brightened the dark recesses beneath the truck.

"Oh no," he moaned. Then, instinctively, Zak pushed up on the truck axle and miraculously moved the vehicle a few inches. With his other hand, he pulled the disheveled figure from under the cab, and the missing phone whirled out.

With haste, Zak called the emergency number while tying a tourniquet to the victim's bleeding leg. He relayed the highway accident location, explaining that they should follow the fresh tractor tracks. He then placed a truck blanket over the unknown casualty.

Bending over, he spoke into the ear of the unfortunate victim, "Listen, old pal, the operator said the emergency crew will be here in ten minutes. There's nothing more I can do anyway, so under the circumstances, I'm going to leave you. There will be a lot of questions I would just as soon not answer."

Zak climbed back upon the Caterpillar to finish burrowing the few remaining yards to the open road, his left arm still electrified. Once on the highway, he whirled the steel juggernaut around and headed back in the direction he came.

CHAPTER 6

When the paramedic team arrived at the local hospital, they repeated a bazaar story told to them by the hallucinatory driver. A short, heavy-set nurse chuckled as she relayed the tale to a group of young interns and nurses of how a tall, masked stranger—whose face the driver could not see—just lifted the truck cab by its axle with one hand. The story brought repeated laughter.

The nurse pointed at her fellow medical assistants, "I'm telling you guys, this patient told me the wildest story to date. But you know, as the tow truck driver took the cab away, he told the paramedics that the axle of that big truck looked like it had been bent by a blow torch. Figure that out."

THE CONFRONTATION

CHAPTER 7
A JOURNEY FULFILLED

Re-tracing the clear tractor tracks, Zak saw that the dozer showed an empty reading on the fuel gauge. "This baby will be dead in the woods in a few minutes. I'll have to jog the rest of the way back," he begrudgingly told himself.

When the steel dozer treads came to a choking halt, Zak leaped from the cab and hit the ground running. His tall, hooded image, engulfed in a haze of black smoke, resembled a ghostly presence. He jogged stealthily forward, heavy condensation puffing from his breath. He could hear sirens, shouting voices, the crackling of fire, and his own heavy cough from the consuming smoke.

Without warning, a vague image appeared before him and partially collided with Zak. Both figures sprawled to the ground. "Whoa mister, didn't see you, pal!" Zak yelled. Springing to his feet, he recognized the white and gold fire chief helmet twirling on the ground. Picking up the helmet and extending a hand to assist the firefighter, Zak spoke first. "We have to quit meeting like this Chief, or we'll never beat this fire.

The chief smiled. "It's you, the guy with the hood. I see you carved a wide swath, and we appreciate it, but what happened to the bulldozer?"

"Ran out of fuel," Zak replied, "I had to abandon it about three miles back. But the break is complete; I made it to the highway."

"I'm Chief Foley. If you want, there's a log church a mile up this new path you've dug. We're using it as a rest center, so help yourself to coffee and maybe some rest. Follow the yellow flags directing the firefighters. I should be there myself in a couple of hours, so maybe I'll see you again. In the meantime, I think we have this inferno under control. Oh, by the way, I put your motorcycle in a small shed behind that church. See ya." Zak watched the chief disappear into the smoke.

Yellow flags nailed to trees pointed the way to the quaint log cabin church. A beautiful hand-carved crucifix stood over the doorway, and underneath, carved letters read: *St. Gabriel of the Woods.* Zak opened the heavy, wooden door, and before him stood an old lighted Catholic alter. Only six rows of pews filled the walls of the premises. He smiled, recalling how long it had been since he had attended church.

To his right, a narrow opening revealed a staircase leading to an underground basement where voices could be heard. Descending the stairs, Zak crouched to enter a cramped room where a weary bunch of firefighters sat at long tables. Most were devouring sandwiches and guzzling beer. A big stainless steel coffee urn perked a noisy brew. Conversations temporarily halted to observe Zak's entrance. Someone yelled, "Get yourself a beer, partner, and the sandwiches are in the refrigerator."

"Thanks," Zak responded. Grabbing a cold beer from a big sink, Zak sat at the closest table.

Engaging in small talk with two men who also said they were volunteers, he listened to harrowing stories of the forest's flaming onslaught. Their conversation was interrupted by a boisterous individual who had clearly consumed too much alcohol. The offender—a giant of a man wearing suspenders over a plaid shirt and bursting at the belly—became increasingly troublesome.

Zak half turned on his bench, wondering if he should intervene when the big guy reached across a table and pulled another man out of his seat.

"Harold, I think it's time I opened your skull to prove there ain't nothing in it," growled the beer-bellied character.

Within seconds, the room rocked in a flurry of benches, tables, and chairs. Others scattered in all directions, hoping to avoid the whirling combatants.

A JOURNEY FULFILLED

"Hold it—hold it, lumberjack!" Zak yelled. He quickly threw a headlock around the plaid-shirted, overstuffed perpetrator. "Ok, big fella, this is a church, and we're all here to get some rest and recuperation, so cut it out, Buster!"

The barrel-chested character dipped his head and whipped his massive shoulders, flipping Zak over and against the logged wall.

A deafening silence fell over the room as Zak slowly pulled himself to his knees. The wild one broke into hysterical laughter, raised his burly arms towards the ceiling, and screamed, "Church, is it? Well, call me fire and brimstone big guy." He rushed at Zak in a maddening fury, his giant fist poised to strike. A ponderous blow struck Zak's arm as he attempted to fend off the encounter. Again, the impact slammed him against the hard, wooden wall.

Dodging sharply in one direction, the offender's next blow missed Zak and thumped against the heavy logs. Zak realized the familiar vibration in his left arm and instantaneously threw a solid punch to the lumberjack's paunchy stomach. The massive hulk groaned loudly and crumbled to the floor in a weighty heap, almost on top of Zak. Zak gazed down at his glowing fist, amazed and shaken by the sight of it.

CHAPTER 7

A few men went to the aid of their drunken comrade. One shouted, "What in God's name did you hit him with, mister?" They unraveled the big hulk to lay him on his back.

"Man," one member of the group said, "I ain't never seen Benji knocked down before, let alone knocked out."

Zak staggered to his feet and sat on a bench. "A lucky punch, I guess. Is he okay?"

"He's out cold, but he's breathing," observed a man who appeared to have some medical knowledge. He checked the fallen battler once more. "He'll be alright, but my word, one punch, and I think he has a couple of broken ribs; funny, do I smell smoke?"

The guy who had been pulled across the table walked over to Zak. "I appreciate your help, mister, but Benji ain't never been beat in a fight before in his life. I don't know who you are or how you did it, but if I were you, I'd hightail it out of here, like now. I know when Benji wakes up, he's going to want to go at it again."

Zak, with his left hand buried deep in his pocket, stood up. "Well, if your friend Benji is going to be all right, tell him I once won a local heavyweight championship tournament. Even if I didn't." He quickly ascended the nearby stairway.

A JOURNEY FULFILLED

Stopping momentarily at the upstairs alter, he stared intently at the fading glow in his hand. He genuflected, made the sign of the cross, mumbled a few words, and scrambled out the church doorway.

Easily finding the small shed at the back of the church, Zak delighted in seeing his road companion, the shiny green Harley Davidson. Rolling the cycle to the path, he quickly mounted the bike, kicked the starter once, and the familiar mellow sound carried him back toward the open road.

As he again cruised along the mountainous road, Zak spoke openly. "Won't be long now, Sam. According to your map, I'll be in Stove Pipe Wells tomorrow. I hope the gold is still there if it is where you say it is."

Powering his way over the Sierra Nevada's and into the great Mojave Desert, he felt a rush of elation thinking about the gold, but couldn't help but wonder; was he chasing an old man's pipe dream or his own?

The desert does strange things to those who invade it, especially at dusk. The heat, radiating from its cooling surface, conjures up make-believe images on the darkening horizon. A variety of optical illusions tease human perception. Holding tightly to the high elbow handlebars, his imagination rambled as fast as the speedy

CHAPTER 7

bike. Again, he hoped to find a place to stay for the night and perhaps make it to Stove Pipe by late tomorrow.

Just after midnight, an arrangement of small individual cottages appeared over the horizon. An oblong, white fluorescent sign read: *Occupancy.* Most of the cottages were empty, so upon registering, Zak chose one isolated from the others.

Moving his motorcycle toward a cabin marked with a big "2" over the door, he was surprised to see another green-colored motorcycle parked in front of another cottage. It bore a distinct resemblance to his Harley. Zak decided to place his bike around the back of his residence. That night, he enjoyed one of the few comfortable nights of sleep he had experienced in a long time.

Checking out early, as bright morning rays infiltrated his sunglasses, Zak noticed through the office window that the other motorcycle had not moved from its spot. "Looks like I have a fellow biker in room four, huh?" he casually remarked to the resort owner.

"Yeah, he's alone too and said he would be checking out last night. You just never know with people traveling the road, especially when they're alone."

"Thanks for the compliment," Zak retorted before walking from the office.

Heading back to his bike and past the almost duplicate cycle, Zak noticed the door of the number 4 cottage was ajar. He looked back at the office and then decided to investigate. Peeking through the small door opening, he called out, "Hey buddy, is everything ok? I mean, your door is open, and—"

Before he could finish his words, a gust of wind blew the door fully open, and a pool of crimson red blood covered a bed and a bullet-riddled body. Zak's senses were jarred.

He stepped toward the room, then suddenly halted as an uneasy feeling hit his gut. Turning quickly, he sprinted to his bike and cranked its engine. Roaring past the office at breakneck speed, he very quickly put a great deal of distance between himself and the scenic cottage resort.

Zak was not sure at first why he was fleeing, but an ominous feeling in his gut told him to run, and to get as far away from that resort as possible. There were too many coincidences for this to just be some random killing. The details were too perfect. The similarities too eerie. The murdered man had the same Harley Davidson as Zak, and was staying at the same hotel, and the way the man was murdered looked intentional and gruesome. It almost looked like the work of a professional.

CHAPTER 7

It soon became clear to Zak that the murderer had in fact mistaken the victim for someone else, and that someone else might be Zak himself. But why, why would someone want to kill Zak? Wracking his brain, the answer suddenly came to him: Teresa's family. The same family that Teresa warned him was dangerous. Pushing the bike to its limit, Zak thought to himself. *Wait 'til the old man finds out they got the wrong guy.*

Stove Pipe Wells has all the appearances of which the name implies. A nondescript, dusty western town situated in the heart of Death Valley. Sam Rooney's map ended in this sunbaked village, and according to its concluding message, a small airport location contained the treasure.

The airport, Yucca Flat, represented an "X" mark on the map. Motoring slowly, Zak quickly located the airport. The final words on Sam's map read:

> *"You'll find a key at the base of the memorial flagpole in the back of the main building. Be certain you read the commemorative plaque at the base. Ask the person at the desk about the key, and you'll know where the gold is."*

A JOURNEY FULFILLED

Sliding from the bike, Zak walked cautiously toward the rusty flagpole in the back of a small terminal building. A ragged flag hung from the thirty-foot structure, and like the message said, a large steel base tripod held the pole steady. In days past, the flag flew proudly before the doors where the original entrance to the building stood. Indeed, a plaque with worn words read: *Dedicated to stand forever, for the six Marines who raised our flag on the battlefield of Iwo Jima.*

"Old Sam wanted to be sure this structure would remain intact," reasoned Zak. Reaching under the base of the pole, his hand groped, finding nothing. "Oh no. Don't tell me this whole thing is a big bust."

He then reached further underneath, through cobwebs and debris, when his hand gripped a small, magnified key box anchored to the underneath of the steel tripod. The tiny black box had rusted, but did slide open, revealing a numbered locker key. Excited, Zak entered the new terminal building.

Directly in front of him stood an information counter, where a uniformed woman stood. "Can I help you sir?" she asked.

He showed her the key. "Yes, could you tell me if you have lockers?"

CHAPTER 7

She smiled. "Have we got lockers? Best in the state! Just follow those blue arrows on the tile floor."

The arrows led Zak to a long row of brightly colored, oversized lockers. Searching for the number 312, he hesitated upon discovering the correct locker. The key fit, and he turned it slowly. A *click* sound snapped the metal door open, and he stood agape.

Four large canvas sacks, all tied with miner's rope, lay before him. Looking around the empty waiting room, he nervously but carefully opened one sack. As he peeked over the top of the canvas opening, Zak's eyes caught the golden sparkle of which only pure gold could reflect.

"Sam, you old coot, you had them all bamboozled," he whispered. Then he remembered the murdered man at the gas station and another at the cottage and he thought to himself about the strange series of events that had unfolded since his accident at the powerlines. It felt to him now that he was on a collision course with a very strange fate. A fate that was now a part of his life whether he wanted it or not.

A JOURNEY FULFILLED

CHAPTER 8
KEEPING A PROMISE

Back on the road, with his two saddle bags bursting from the weight of Sam's extraordinary bounty, Zak contemplated the prospect of a long journey through the Midwest to an obscure town in Minnesota.

Heading east, and stopping for gas at Indian Springs, Nevada, a newspaper headline inside a news box caught his eye. It read: *Reputed Mob Figures Maniatis Brothers Slain.* Purchasing a paper, he sat at an adjacent diner to read the startling story.

Accounts told of what appeared to be a typical inter-mob style assassination of Ron and Morrow Maniatis in a bleak area of the Mojave Desert. Both bodies had been hog-tied, buried, and shot in the head three times each. The classic signs of empty pockets—apart from one penny—established an age-old mob tradition.

The story covered two pages, relating the history of the powerful and infamous Maniatis family. It concluded with a mention of the only two living members of the family remaining: the notorious godfather himself, Philip Maniatis, and his daughter Teresa. Concern over possible mob infighting over control of the vast Las Vegas holdings infiltrated the report.

Finishing a cup of coffee, Zak looked out over the irrepressible desert. He weighed the possibilities of taking a detour through Vegas and sharing a moment of consolation with Teresa Maniatis. Interstate 93 would take him directly through the gambling mecca.

"Why not," he concluded. Jumping aboard the dusty Harley, he headed toward the glittering swank of the Las Vegas Strip.

Arriving at night, Zak drove through the main drag of the gambling epicenter. He saw the town as a huge pinball machine as he rolled by the gaming palaces, zapping each as he passed.

This place should have been called simply, "Glitz," he thought.

It did not take long to find that the Maniatis family owned seven of the most popular casinos, and that Philip Maniatis usually maintained an office penthouse suite in a lavish structure called "The Pharaoh."

Finding a daily storage operation with appropriate security measures, Zak garaged the motorcycle and its precious cargo. He walked to the nearest stoplight and hailed an approaching taxi.

"Cabby, how close are we to The Pharaoh?"

CHAPTER 8

"Get in, mister, you'll be losing your money in ten minutes," the cab driver chuckled.

Entering the elaborate surroundings of music, lights, and the grid of slot machines, Zak inquired about Mr. Maniatis' residence. A mini-skirted showgirl directed him to an isolated area and a private elevator. In front of that elevator door stood what appeared to be a mannequin at first, but in fact, was an overdressed fat man in a shiny green double-breasted suit.

Zak approached the robust character. "Excuse me, but I would like to see Mr. Maniatis," he asked.

"Sure, buddy, so would a thousand other people," replied the caustic guardian of the elevator.

Zak partly turned his head, then looked down at the floor before speaking. "Do yourself a favor, friend, and just tell your boss the man with the hood is here."

A puzzled look twisted the dark face of the green-suited watchdog. He walked straight up to stare into Zak's face, his eyes narrowing as he spoke through a smattering of missing teeth.

"If he ain't heard of the jerk with the hood, pal, I'm going to stuff that bonnet down your throat." Begrudgingly, he dialed from a portable phone. "Tell Mr. M that there's a guy here with a hood that wants to see him," he said.

KEEPING A PROMISE

After a brief pause, the pudgy bodyguard shrugged his shoulders. "You must have the magic word, pal. The elevator will take you to its only stop, so see the man; so, don't make any wrong turns, you got it?"

Inside the small elevator, two obvious surveillance cameras assured Zak his presence was being closely observed. A claustrophobic sense within the steel monitored cube bothered him. The elevator stopped, and a sliding door slowly opened to an elaborate suite of exquisitely designed furnishings.

At the far end of the room sprawled a glistening mahogany desk. Seated behind the oversized desk, Zak recognized the petite and extremely attractive Teresa Maniatis.

"Teresa!" he exclaimed, "something tells me that desk is just a little too big for such a tiny woman."

She stood up, smiled, and brushing away her blond hair, came from behind the barrier. "Zak, what a pleasant surprise it is to see you again." The two embraced each other. "I'm sure you have heard of our tragic circumstances, and I do appreciate your coming."

"Yes, and I wish to express my condolences to you and your family," he replied softly.

"Which now consists only of my father and me, I'm sad to say," she stammered, sitting on the edge of the desk. "On top of that...I lost the baby."

Zak looked at Teresa grimly. "You've had your share of tragedies. Are there any suspects or indications of how your brothers' deaths came about?"

She walked back to the heavy-leathered desk chair with her head down. "No, only that there is some evidence that points to an act of revenge toward my father. If you recall, Zak, I mentioned that there were dangerous elements with my family's operations."

Zak continued his stare. "Teresa, I'm well aware of your family's infamous history of reputed underworld activities."

Walking around the desk to sit and taking an authoritative stance, Teresa looked back sternly at Zak, her voice firm and clear. "I guess it all comes with the territory, huh Zak?"

"Could be," he replied. Suddenly, a side door opened and the familiar electric wheelchair of Mr. Philip Maniatis bumped against the door opening.

His deep, hearse voice gravitated as he spoke. "Curses, I always find it difficult to navigate this doorway. Well, the mystery man with a guarded face, this is a pleasant surprise." His wheelchair moved in spurts in Zak's direction, his hand extended in greeting.

As he shook his hand, Zak spoke. "Mr. Maniatis, I'm so sorry about your sons, and I hope the perpetrators are soon apprehended."

Philip Maniatis dropped his gaze then looked up through reddened, narrow eyes. "I have no doubt they will be found and that my sons' deaths will be avenged, Mr. Zak, and I thank you."

Rolling his wheelchair to the side of the big desk, the chieftain of the Vegas gambling empire broke into a big smile. "Mr. Zak, what do you think of my little ninety-pound kitten Teresa taking over where her old man left off? I'm not getting any younger, you know, and this wheelchair does put me in somewhat of a vulnerable position."

Zak looked at Teresa and partly smiled. "Mr. Maniatis, I'm beginning to believe that neither of you knows what the word vulnerable means. On that note, I'll leave you two moguls to your maneuvering and money counting." Zak rose from his chair and continued, "My intentions were to say hello and offer my sympathies, but I think saying take care of yourselves is more meaningful."

CHAPTER 8

Walking back to the elevator door, Zak turned to look at Teresa again. "Teresa, congratulations on your promotion. I'm having trouble digesting it right now, but I'm sure you and your father know what you're doing. Shows you how wrong a guy can be."

The elevator door opened, and Zak stepped inside.

"Hold that door a minute, Mr. Zak," ordered Mr. Maniatis, "I want to express again my appreciation for your aid to Teresa." He reached a crippled hand into his suit's side pocket. "Please accept this small favor as a token of my thanks. As you can see, it's a casino chip, and I ask that while you pass the roulette table on your way out, you simply place the five-hundred-dollar blue chip on number thirty-two red."

Maniatis pushed a side button on the hi-tech wheelchair, carrying him quickly to Zak's side. He placed the gambling chip in Zak's pocket. On command, the wheelchair backed up, and the elevator door closed.

As he reached the main floor, Zak looked at the uncommon blue chip.

I wonder, is it possible that his authoritative power could extend to this small, glistening disc, like some computer chip?

As expected, the roulette table stood directly in the path of his departure. He approached the mass of gamblers surrounding the brightly lit table and stopped at the table's edge. Between the verbal hawking and the brightly dressed patrons partially submerged in cigarette smoke, it all looked like something he had seen out of a movie. He placed his hand on the green felt cover and stared at the multitude of block red and black numbers on the surface.

Zak's presence went unnoticed as he slowly placed the unique chip on thirty-two. The club roller, in circus fashion, barked out betting jargon and spun the big, colorful roulette wheel.

Before Zak could adjust to his uncomfortable surroundings, voices yelled, "Red thirty-two, it's red thirty-two!"

The table manager pushed a large stack of winnings over Zak's lone chip that covered his bet. "Nice piece of luck for a new customer, mister" he quipped.

Everyone at the table turned to observe the lucky character in the strange, hooded sweatshirt. Zak calmly shoved the pile of chips into his slit pockets and claimed a hefty seventeen thousand dollar return at the cash-in window.

"Who said we should beware of Greeks bearing gifts," he chucked to himself.

CHAPTER 8

Exiting The Pharaoh Casino, Zak deftly descended the many marble stairs cascading to the street. A dark limousine pulled up in front of him, cutting his progress.

The driver, displaying a heavy mustache, spoke to him. "Got a free taxi for you, buddy. Hop in."

At the same moment, another man came out of the passenger side, walked around the car, and approached Zak. "Yeah, imagine that stranger. A free Rolls Royce taxi, and you can sit in front too." The black steel barrel of a .357 Magnum revolver protruded from his cashmere coat. Smiling broadly, he motioned with the gun in mock politeness. "Please, be my guest, won't you? I insist."

Zak looked at the driver, who also brandished a gun. "Something free in Las Vegas, I guess it's an offer I can't refuse," he answered.

He sat in the front passenger seat of the car while the man in the dark coat took a position in the back.

The powerful, almost silent Rolls Royce engine moved the limousine swiftly through the crowded, glimmering strip. Without turning his head, Zak asked, "I don't suppose your instructions include telling me where we're going and for how long?"

"No problem, we thought you might like to share our culture trip to explore Hoover Dam, ain't that right Gustav?" the man in the back answered.

Zak, trying desperately not to lose his head, replied, "I don't mean to be ungrateful, fellas, but I've already been to that world wonder. So, if I can save you and myself the time, money, and gasoline in this sleeper car, we can call it a night now."

"Very funny, wise guy," the driver responded, "but this trip is a mandatory, once-in-a-lifetime deal. Heck, you might not want to ever come back from where you're going, so relax, Mr. Cool"

It did not take long for the desert's darkness to envelop them. Only the bright headlights projected, like camera beams in a cinema. A narrow road blurred ahead of them, and only the thumping sounds of evenly spaced tar strips broke the silence. Zak's mind whirled in disarray as he attempted to weigh the precarious situation and how he could establish an escape.

His captors had ceased talking, creating a dramatic atmosphere of long silence. Sweat beads trickled down Zak's heavily lined face. His instincts tingled in expectation of some lethal onslaught.

A slight ruffling sound from behind alarmed his senses, and before the piano wire could tear through his neck, Zak's quick reflexes caught the steel barb with one finger. He had lodged the finger of his left hand between the deadly wire loop and his neck.

CHAPTER 8

The assassin in the back growled, "It's all over, sucker," as he pulled the wire noose tighter.

Instinctively, Zak brought his feet up to the windshield, kicking in furious desperation, when the familiar blue glow of his hand filled the car's compartment. The wire's noose lit up in a blinding flash, bringing an unreal scream from the hoodlum in the back seat.

A strong smell of burnt cashmere prevailed. The driver, agape, reached for his revolver, which Zak quickly clenched with his emblazoned hand. The driver's eyes bulged, and his mouth opened, but no sound came from him. He wrenched, then stiffened and crumbled against the steering wheel. The Rolls Royce jolted and veered off the road, throwing all occupants violently to the floor.

Jammed between the floorboard and the driver's body, Zak felt dizzy as the huge car careened wildly through the desert terrain. Then, as though it had hit a brick wall, the limousine came to an abrupt halt. It almost turned over before bogging down in the deep, soft sand; its precision engine roared and died.

Except for the electrostatic crackle emanating from Zak's bluish hand, it was silent. Rolling over the entangled body of the driver and wiggling up to a sitting position in the front seat, Zak caught his breath and surveyed the aftermath. In the black of night, only the eerie, blue ember from his hand beaconed a view.

The crumpled passenger door would not open, so Zak forcefully threw his body against it until it gave way. Upon opening, he tumbled to the ground. The sand was cold and appeared unusually soft. As expected, the front wheels of the car were mired deeply into a mound of sand.

On his knees, Zak stared at his trembling translucent hand. There appeared to be a stream of blue, green, and white tentacles running within his inner skin.

How freakish this phenomenon is, he thought, *how unexplainable, and yet so powerful.*

Rising to his feet, Zak remembered the instance during the forest fire when he partially lifted the overturned truck. He placed his glowing hand under the front fender of the Rolls Royce and easily lifted the vehicle from the soft earth.

After laying both bodies on the extended rear floor of the limo, Zak started the engine and backed the car onto the highway. The engine sounded rough, but he managed to reach high speeds as he headed back to Las Vegas.

Arriving back in the gambling mecca, Zak parked the dusty and crumpled Rolls Royce directly in front of The Pharaoh Casino. He walked to Mr. Maniatis' private elevator and again was confronted by the obnoxious bodyguard.

"Tell your boss his two goons are out front, and that the next time he sends someone to do a job, they'll get burned badly."

KEEPING A PROMISE

CHAPTER 9
THE UNEXPECTED

After paying the rental fee at the storage garage, Zak reclaimed his Harley-Davidson and the gold, packed safely in the locked saddlebags. He knew it was best that he leave town immediately. The warm night air streaming across his face felt good as he roared out onto the highway once again. Zak took a northerly course on route 93 and decided to drive a long haul before finding a comfortable place to stay. He could use a day or two of much-needed contemplation.

After eight hours of desert and foothill driving, he approached a town called Indian Springs. There, he discovered a sprawling bed and breakfast establishment named Red's. Carrying the heavy saddlebags over his shoulders, Zak secured a two-room accommodation. He placed the bags containing the gold under the king-size bed and fell into a long sleep.

In the morning, Zak joined eight guests at Red's oval breakfast table and engaged in conversation with a gentleman who claimed to own a used car business nearby. He called himself Mr. Mickey, "The man with the backward K," as he put it. He proudly displayed a silver-colored calling card, which proved his name was, in fact, spelled with a backward "K".

As he smoked a cigar, Mickey gestured to Zak. "Listen, Zak, call me Mick—the guy who wants you to trade in that green Harley-Davidson I saw you cruise in with. I've got a classic, green '69 Pontiac GTO convertible on my lot that you might want to talk about."

Biting into a strawberry raisin sweet roll, Zak smiled and spoke with mild interest. "Mick, I think you know my cycle is a bit of a classic too, and unless your GTO is like new, you might be taking advantage of me."

"No way, friend," countered the man with a backward "K" in his name, "this convertible comes with low miles, and I had no intentions of selling it until I saw your bike. I'm a sucker for those old Harley dogs."

Zak, knowing that Maniatis and his thugs would be on the lookout for a traveler on a green Harley, thought this was the perfect opportunity to ditch the bike. "Mr. Backward K, I actually might need a roof over my head, even if it is canvas. Tell me how to get to your car lot, and I'll meet you there after breakfast."

That car lot, adorned in colorful pennants, proved to be only minutes from the inn, and Zak could not miss

CHAPTER 9

the GTO Micky had talked about. Displayed high on a slow revolving ramp in front of the used car operation, the sparkling green convertible appeared to be in showroom condition. He parked his Harley-Davidson in front of the sales office and approached Mickey, who wore a Mexican sombrero and was sunning himself on a small deck attached to the office.

"Mr. Backward K, I admire decisiveness, so without examining your GTO or you inspecting my Harley, let's make it an even trade, no questions asked."

Mickey moved from his lounge chair, a quizzical look on his face. "You mean, just like that?" he asked, extinguishing his cigar.

Zak held out his hand. "Just a simple handshake, Mr. Mickey. Maybe the first old-fashioned, above-board deal you've made in a long time."

Mickey laughed, "Never, in fact." He hesitated, then meekly shook Zak's hand. "I don't believe this, Zak, and I haven't even seen your face with that droopy hood. But I'm going to do it and tell my friends this story until I'm old and grey, and maybe broke."

Zak held his keys up high. "Mickey, I just had these made in Vegas a few days ago."

They exchanged keys while Mickey had the GTO removed from the ramp. Zak sat down on a nearby bench. "Mick, I don't have a title to give you, but you have my word that the person I acquired this Harley from is no longer looking for it."

Mickey sat down beside him. "No problem, Zak. The title I'm giving you, shall we say, contains a few blank spaces you can fill in yourself, and for a while, you can use the dealer plates."

They both stood up with equally dubious smiles on their faces. "I think if I knew the significance of that backward "K" thing, I wouldn't do this," Zak remarked. "See ya, Mick." He stepped into the Pontiac GTO convertible, waved, and sped away.

After packing the sacks containing the gold securely into the trunk of his newly acquired convertible, Zak decided to check out of Red's bed and breakfast a day early. The car seemed to run well as he moved swiftly on the highway. The big, V8 engine sounded smooth and roared as boldly as the Harley Davidson.

A day later, a severe rainstorm swept the roadway, and Zak felt relieved that he had traded the motorcycle. Pellets of heavy rain pounded the car's canvas top as he skirted the Ruby Mountain ridges. Up ahead, the familiar red glow of an emergency flare splashed through his fast-moving windshield wipers, signifying trouble.

CHAPTER 9

Nearing the point of where the flares had been placed, Zak saw a nun wearing a traditional habit, and a priest with a yellow umbrella, standing alongside a disabled school bus. The black and yellow vehicle had apparently been run off the road, its passenger area wedged between a ditch and the edge of the mountain. The middle-aged nun approached Zak's car in frustration.

"Oh, sir, we have seven children inside our crippled bus and an injured Sister. Could you offer some assistance in contacting help from the closest emergency facility?"

"Sister, I would be happy to help. Are there any serious injuries?" Zak asked.

"I think possibly Sister Julie, who had been standing at the front of the bus when it careened over the embankment. She was thrown hard against the windshield and was knocked unconscious, so we put her on the seat in the bus."

Leaving his car, Zak observed a badly bruised face. A bluish color had already spread across her young features, and blood had caked on the side of her tightly fit habit.

Zak turned to the priest. "Father, I didn't think the nuns wore these hoods, or habits, anymore. In any case, I'm going to have to remove this headpiece to examine the extent of her injury."

Father McBride nodded affirmatively. "Sir, please forgive our strict order, and do whatever you can to help Sister Julie."

As Zak gently removed the nun's habit, a rush of long, dark hair trickled around her bruised but attractive face.

Wow, not at all like the nuns I remember in grammar school.

It became apparent to Zak that the young lady, who they called Sister Julie, had suffered a concussion, a shoulder separation, and possibly other internal injuries.

"Father McBride, your sister needs hospital attention immediately. If you'd like, I'll take her back to Indian Springs to the hospital I recall seeing. Maybe you can spare the other nun in accompanying us?"

"I'll ask Sister Valento to join you, and we'll pray that you send assistance back for the rest of us as soon as possible. God speed," answered Father McBride.

Carrying the tiny nun out of the bus and up the embankment, Zak related his intentions to Sister Valento.

She answered softly, "I will stay here, sir, the children need my help now. We have to rely on your benevolence and have faith that you will keep our sister safe. May the Lord be with you, one who shields his face."

CHAPTER 9

"Sister Valento, in my years of parochial education, I have never disobeyed a nun; I'm not going to start now. You'll hear from Sister Julie or me within two days."

The rain had subsided as Zak gently placed the unconscious nun in the back seat of the Pontiac. After he turned the car around, he put the GTO to the test. Traveling at speeds over one hundred miles per hour on a rain-slick highway. The car fared well.

Zak skid the brakes outside the emergency entrance of the small Indian Springs Hospital, startling the doctors and nurses standing near the doorway. They shuffled outside to intercept Zak as he carried the disheveled nun.

He watched as the medical team placed her on a rolling stretcher. "She had an accident while onboard a school bus. You should send back help, on route 93 to Ruby Ridge," Zak yelled.

An attendant placed a hand on Zak's shoulder and calmly answered him. "We'll have ambulances out there immediately. Right now, have some coffee in the waiting room. You can fill us in on the details, and we'll keep you informed of the patient's condition."

"Thanks," Zak responded, then walked slowly into the empty waiting room. While he sat, he mulled over the difficult circumstances.

THE UNEXPECTED

Maybe I should just leave now and save myself from interrogation. I could head back to Red's and call in the morning, but something compels me to stay and see if this woman will be okay.

"Mister, hey mister, wake up," was the next thing Zak heard as he uncurled himself from sleep on a leather sofa. An attendant jostled his shoulder and spoke softly. "The nun has regained consciousness sir, and she would like to see you. She's in room 101."

He hustled down a long hallway and entered the designated room. In a half-seated position, Sister Julie turned her bandaged head to face Zak. "Are you my benefactor, mister...?" she questioned.

"Zak. Just plain Zak, Sister. And yes, if that's what you call it, but I'm only the one who drove you to the hospital. How are you?"

"Fine, thank you, Zak, although I am waiting for the results of my CAT scan."

Zak could not help but be affected by this young nun's extraordinary beauty. Her long, raven hair was splashed against the white pillows, accentuating her flawless olive skin, and striking emerald eyes. He felt slightly embarrassed to be having these feeling about a nun.

"Zak, the children, Sister Valento, and Father McBride...are they okay?"

CHAPTER 9

"Only you suffered an injury, Sister, everyone else is fine. Get some rest, you took a serious blow to the head. Just let the medical professionals handle everything. I'll be leaving here in a few minutes since I have a long journey east, but in a day or two I'll call the hospital to confirm your recovery."

At that moment, a tall doctor entered, carrying a large envelope containing a CAT scan film. "Sister, I'm Doctor Steiner, a man of directness," the gaunt physician asserted as he walked to her bedside, his concise demeanor apparent. "The CAT scan shows a fracture of the skull, as well as what appears to be the formation of a cyst." He quickly pulled a small chair to her side and sat down, his hand combing through his partially balding white hair.

"I recommend an MRI Scan, which would be more definitive. That means you'll have to go to St. James Hospital in Twin Falls, Idaho, which is a good five hundred miles from here. Since both of our ambulatory vehicles are assigned to the Ruby Mountain incident, I must ask this good Samaritan gentleman," he looked at Zak, "to accommodate us."

Zak looked back at the impressive doctor. "Doctor, if that's your professional opinion, let's get this woman into my car. We should be at St. James in less than five hours."

THE UNEXPECTED

The doctor stood up and shook Julie's hand. "Sister, I do not think it's life-threatening, so don't let this character set a world speed record. We'll phone ahead and inform the hospital of your coming."

With the accelerator to the floor, Zak put his newly acquired car to the ultimate test. The hospital personnel had constructed a comfortable makeshift bed in the back seat of the cramped Pontiac. A winding trail of dust billowed behind the loud exhausts. A bleak terrain of sand and rocky surfaces surrounding the narrow, but clear, highway allowed for full-throttle driving.

Sister Julie, tucked under a comforter and dressed in borrowed hospital pajamas, maintained a congenial attitude. Zak continued to glance back at her from the rearview mirror. A wistful smile crossed her face. "Zak, I must confess, I've always had a fantasy about driving a race car in the Indianapolis 500 Mile Speedway. Looks like my dream might be coming partly true."

Zak laughed. "Sister, I don't want to take any chances. The problem in your skull might be a lot worse than Doctor Steiner diagnosed. If you can, get some rest, we should be getting the checkered flag in a couple of hours."

By nightfall, Zak became alarmed when the dashboard temperature gauge bordered close to the warning red line.

CHAPTER 9

A slight, rough engine sound also indicated a possible overheating development.

"I hope this extra-clean, used car Mickey convinced me of wasn't originally painted yellow for *lemon*," he murmured to himself.

Early morning rays cast an orange glow on the metallic profile of the sleek GTO, as it now moved more slowly on the desolate road. Turning the heater on and cruising at a slower speed, Zak attempted to conserve on the overheating dilemma while continuing to move.

As he kept his eyes on the road ahead, Zak broke the silence. "Sister, I'm sorry to say we have a heating problem, so I'll have to slow down a bit. Maybe if we're lucky a repair shop of some kind will come into view."

"Whatever, Zak," she answered, "we have what you call 'the man upstairs' keeping a close watch on us."

Zak turned slightly; a cynical smile formed across his concerned face.

Only moments after Sister Julie spoke, Zak reacted with astonishment at the sight of a small, dust-covered gas station appearing over the horizon. Two ancient gas pumps stood in front of what appeared to be an abandoned operation. But as the steam-wrenching Pontiac pulled into the dilapidated driveway, the front door creaked open. An elderly man wearing bib overalls and sprouting a grey beard stepped from the adobe shack.

"Looks like the return of Stanley Steamer to me," the man remarked. "Better pull the hood, driver, and keep that engine running while I try to get some water into the radiator."

Zak pulled the hood latch and stepped from the car. "Much obliged, mister. I figured we were not too long from being stranded in the desert."

"That's what a lot of people say when they stop at Old Crow's Way Station," replied the attendant.

Using a homemade steel pole with a movable claw at the end, the aged gentleman removed the radiator cap, creating a roar of steam belching upward. Immediately pouring water from a hose attached to an old water tank, the steam quickly subsided.

"Nothing like a cool drink of water, even for a slick hot rod, huh partner? Maybe you'll let me drive this green hornet sometime," the old-timer quipped.

Zak anxiously spoke, "I have an injured person resting in the back seat, as you can see. With a bum radiator, I won't get far. Do you know of any way we can find help in getting to St. James Hospital?"

Holding the straps of his overalls, the attendant walked over to the back of the car and peered through the window. Sister Julie waved in a gesture of appreciation. "With all those head bandages, it looks like the young lady should be getting to St. James mighty quick," he responded.

Still gripping his overall straps, he walked slowly over to Zak. "Guess it's time to take to the air, stranger. If you look outback, that's a runway. There's only one, but a good crosswind pilot like me can take off like an astronaut. A litter further east," he pointed in a direction obscured by blowing sand, "if you look hard enough, you'll see an old barn. That's where I keep my pride and joy, my Cessna 177. I can see the doubt in your shadowy eyes, but no fear my friend, my wrinkled face, as you can see, is minus glasses. Maybe everything else is fading, but I've been blessed with hawk eyes. We can arrange for my partner, Luke, to order and replace your GTO radiator while we're gone. It's going to cost you, but it'll also save you and that wounded young lady a heck of a lot of time."

Zak started back toward the car, his words sharp, "You've got a deal, partner, if I can leave some of my personal luggage in that big safe I see just inside the door."

"No problem," the old man returned.

"You open the safe," Zak continued, "and make whatever phone calls you need to, then get that Cessna warmed up; I'll meet you at the runway."

Loading the sacks of gold into the large, steel-constructed safe and closing the six-inch thick steel door, Zak proceeded to park his car inside the small garage. He then informed Sister Julie of their situation.

Smiling, she responded in her typical, optimistic fashion, "Oh, Zak, I think it might be a stroke of luck. We could be in Twin Falls in less than an hour. I'm sorry to be such a burden, but I'm also very grateful."

He positioned himself in the back seat area, carefully picking up Sister Julie and her bed clothing. "Sister, you're as light as a feather, so let's head for the skies."

The compact yellow and white Cessna sat at the end of the lone runway, its engine idling a finely tuned sound. As Zak approached, carrying his patient, the small door to the aircraft swung open.

"By the way, my name is Roy," shouted the attendant and part-time pilot.

"Roy, I'm Zak, and this is Sister Julie," replied Zak, "put the throttle to this beauty and set your course for Twin Falls."

Waves of morning heat gave assistance to the perky aircraft as it rose quickly against the sun's bright rays.

Roy, obviously enjoying his smooth takeoff, commented, "Did you say, Sister Julie, Zak? You mean a religious sister, like a nun?"

"Keep your eyes on the altimeter and the horizon, Roy. Sister Julie is our good luck charm."

Thirty minutes into a smooth flight, a radio transmission blared out a brief message: "Cessna CN 402, this is Twin Falls Tower. Weather conditions approaching from the mountains due west indicate a potential storm watch. Please be advised to maintain this coordinate on a frequent basis. Over."

Roy returned with a message of concurrence. Sister Julie commented, "Anything wrong with a communication like that, Roy?"

"Weathermen were born to worry, Sister, and this little buggy was built for tough times," Roy assured her.

"Did some flying myself," lamented Zak, "mostly opened cockpit and a brief encounter with stunt flying. But that was a long time ago Roy, so I can be your trusty co-pilot."

"Hey, a flyboy," Roy remarked, "maybe we can tell bomber jacket stories over a beer in Twin Falls," they laughed.

Two more radio communications from Twin Falls suggested a possible change in their flight plans.

THE UNEXPECTED

Comments from the Twin Falls Tower explained that weather conditions could dictate an alternate landing destination.

"Gosh darn it—excuse me, Sister," snorted Roy, "of all times for an unlikely snow squall to slip out of nowhere in the mountains."

Radio transmissions became more frequent and discerning as the small Cessna began to buffet against unexpected wind sheers. Visibility quickly diminished, and an atmosphere of growing concern prevailed in the cockpit.

"Even this radio static is increasing," griped Roy.

Zak intently peered out the now obliterated windows. "Well, so much for being able to see anything," he surmised. "Roy, I hope we're high enough to avoid any nearby mountains. If you know our position, it might be time to let Twin Falls know. If you feel like you can bring this baby down while we're still near level ground, maybe it's worth a shot."

Roy, with composure, looked forward and replied, "Zak, I'm having trouble maintaining altitude, so I have to go down and take a look."

Sister Julie interjected, "Gentlemen, I thought my bus at Ruby Ridge would go over the edge of the mountain at one time. One more tempt at fate is just another test of my intestinal fortitude. I can't fly the plane, I even get airsick, so I leave our fate in your hands, and yes, someone else's too."

Roy sent out a radio distress message. "This is Cessna CN 402 calling Twin Falls Tower. We're thirty minutes south of you, out of Ruby Ridge. This is a May Day, May Day. Over."

After continually repeating the distress call, they received only loud static. Sister Julie had forced herself up into a sitting position, and both Zak and Roy placed their faces against the windshield.

"It's a complete white-out," came Zak's strained voice.

"If you see anything, Zak, let me know," Roy urged.

Then, it appeared. Like the calm in the center of a hurricane, a momentary opening of clarity.

"Yikes!" screamed Roy, "look at that, Zak, it looks like a clearing and a ridge of some kind. Whatever it is, it's covered with snow and appears to have enough distance for a possible landing. Everybody prepare for a rough go. Tighten your seatbelts, and you, Sister, count those prayer beads; I'm going to bring this baby down."

Sooner than expected, a whirlwind of blinding snow, the roar of a laborious sounding engine, and some unknown noises were upon them. They tossed about in a roller coaster of snow. Helplessly skidding through a wall of white, they felt a severe jolt, followed by an abrupt stillness. A stinging cold engulfed them, accompanied by a harsh white-out of whistling, biting winds.

The faint voice of Zak came from a mound of snow filling the tattered Cessna compartment. "Sister Julie, Roy, are you ok?" But neither replied. Crawling over debris, he frantically dug away a mound of heavy slush and ice that covered Sister Julie.

He stared at his hand and could feel the vibration in his arm returning. "Here comes the blue ghost again." The eerie blue glow began to stream from his hand. Observing the curled-up figure of Sister Julie, Zak searched for a pulse. "She's alive but unconscious. I hope that's true of Roy," he muttered.

At the twisted controls sat the limp, comatose body of Roy, partly pinned beneath the shattered instrument panel. Zak reached under the panel with his electric arm, easily pulling the entire metal section up. A groan came from Roy's mouth as the heavy pressure released.

"I'm fine, Zak," blurted Sister Julie. "Except for another terrible headache, and I'm still strapped to the backseat."

"Great to hear your voice, Sister," came Zak's relieved reply. "I'll be with you in a minute. It's Roy, Sister, he's out cold, but he's breathing. He's jammed under the instrument panel, so I'm going to try and extricate him."

Undoing Roy's seatbelt and harness, Zak gently dragged Roy from under the front portion of the plane's crumpled interior and laid him between the two front seats.

"Looks like old Roy picked up some of your head bruises, Sister, along with a bad gash to the jaw. Some badly bruised legs, too, which I hope aren't broken from this steering post."

Another groan came from Roy, and Zak went to Sister Julie. "I'll say it before you do, Sister; somebody up there must like all three of us."

"Zak," she clutched his collar, "I know you think being a nun I conjure up obsessive religious beliefs and visions, but I do think—" she hesitated, "providence has assisted us. As God as my judge, when I gained consciousness, I saw a strange blue light glowing in the cockpit. I swear I did; you must believe me."

Zak looked at her strangely. "Sister, I saw it too. Sometimes in catastrophic conditions, people can experience strange illusions."

THE UNEXPECTED

CHAPTER 10
AGAINST THE ODDS

Upon surveying their precarious surroundings, Zak realized the airplane had burrowed through the snow, leaving them partially entombed in a mammoth snowdrift.

"It's cold, and that wind sound means we're not completely covered," he concluded. "I'm going to try and extricate myself from this cabin and explore our situation Sister, keep a close tab on Roy, and if he comes to, ask him about the radio and find out if it's repairable. I'll be back in a few minutes."

Slamming his body repeatedly against the small cockpit door, Zak succeeded in edging himself out of the compartment. As he crawled on his hands and knees through the snow tunnel left by the plane's high-speed impact, he reached a ridge of the mountain. It was much higher than he realized, and all he could see was a blurry scattering of hills surrounded by snow.

"Darn it!" he shouted. "Darkness and snow are coming fast, and I hear the sound of a plane. And wouldn't you know it, I feel the vibration in my arm again."

In the darkening skies overhead, a twin-engine Beechcraft cruised above the point of impact of the buried Cessna. A husband and a wife team piloting the Beechcraft engaged in casual conversation, lamenting their money losses at the Las Vegas casinos.

"Tom," the female companion asserted, staring out the cockpit window, "maybe I've played too many slot machines, but do you see what I see?"

Her pilot husband leaned over to share her view and blinked his eyes twice. "Sharon, it's all desert under that blanket of snow. What kind of light could penetrate that darkness? It looks like someone is waving a blue neon beam; what the heck could it be? Radio our position to Twin Falls and tell them about the weird blue light."

He looked again with his nose against the window and shook his head. "Thank God we both see whatever it is, or I'd give up drinking for good."

Having torn away his shirt sleeve, Zak looked up into the black, snow-flaked sky, waving his glowing arm. "I think they're circling closer to get a fix on our position. I can't see them, but if I'm right, a search party may be back by morning."

Staggering back to the crash scene, Zak informed Sister Julie and the now conscious Roy of the possible rescue. He became concerned, however, when Roy reported that the radio had been demolished and that he had no feeling in his injured legs.

Zak examined Roy's motionless limbs. "Roy, I think both legs have multi-fractures. Since we're stuck in this cold snow tunnel without communications, I'm going to put together a makeshift sled so that we can hopefully reach a warmer low ground."

"And me, with only a double-barrel headache, I can help," urged Sister Julie.

When morning light blanketed the snow-capped peaks, Zak and Sister Julie used the Cessna door as a crude sled and carefully maneuvered it down the mountainside. They strapped Roy on the makeshift toboggan with ropes they had found in the plane's cargo bay. His impassive face reflected the grave prospects ahead.

Barely visible from beneath the layers of blankets, Ray exhorted, "Zak, Sister, you two could do a lot better if you left me here, maybe under some overhang or cave, and went on for help.

Without looking back, Zak grimaced, "Not a chance, Roy. You have the combination to that safe containing all my money, and you also promised to get my GTO in top running condition."

Blizzard conditions began to threaten their plight after only an hour of descending the mountainous terrain. Blinding snow soon brought all movement to a halt.

Spotting a cave-like opening in a rugged section of granite, Zak motioned to Sister Julie. "Sister, that narrow crevice looks like possible shelter. We're not getting anywhere, so let's give it a try until we get a break in this quagmire."

Barely visible through a white veil of snow, Sister Julie waved her hand in the affirmative.

Sudden quietness in the dark cave magnified their unsteady movements. Pulling the cabin door carrying Roy, Zak exerted all his strength to drag the imitation sled over a damp, rocky surface. Sister Julie, exhausted, backed gently against the cave wall and fell into a seated position, gasping.

"Zak, oh Zak, I apologize for my failure to assist you at this critical time, but I'm afraid my strength has abandoned me."

After securing a level spot for Roy, Zak crawled to Sister Julie's side.

Looking at her with admiration he said, "Sister, you've been fine, we couldn't have made it this far without your assistance. Now that we have shelter, we have a chance, and maybe the weather will let up."

Using a flashlight from the plane's emergency box, Zak surveyed the cave interior. Not able to completely stand up, he reacted to an odor, a scattering of small bones, and some fur parts.

"I'd say we've imposed on an animal's sanctuary. I think we're crashing a bear's refuge or maybe a big cat. Whatever, I just hope the critter has an alternate winter residence."

A groan from Roy brought Zak again to his side. "What is it, Roy, are you having pain?"

Almost inaudibly, Roy stammered, "Zak, seven, eleven, box car six, and snake eyes two…that's the safe combination, and…" After a long pause, he continued, "I'll pass on the ride in the GTO." A small trickle of blood came from his nose.

"Roy, Roy," Zak cried, placing his hand to Roy's neck to feel for a pulse. "My God Sister, he's gone; there must have been some internal bleeding."

Sister Julie knelt beside Roy, her hands in prayer, her lips moving in silent words. Zak stumbled toward the cave entrance, tears forming in his eyes, watching the howling snow lash at their refuge. "Sister, we'll cover him on the sled with whatever material we can spare and get his body off this mountain."

Sister Julie touched Zak's shoulder, "Zak, he's safe now, and in good hands, so don't let that which you have no control over trouble you. We may need as many clothing and blankets as possible. Maybe by morning, the storm will subside, and we can reach safety; Roy would want it that way."

Placing Roy's remains near the cave entrance, Zak and Sister Julie's attempt at sleep proved difficult, periodically waking whenever unfamiliar sounds permeated their eerie cavern. Turning restlessly in his tightly wrapped blanket, Zak jolted when he saw two yellow eyes piercing the inky black surroundings. Frozen in fear, he realized the animal—probably a mountain lion–had returned to his or her lair.

Zak attempted to move imperceptibly as he edged from his coverings toward the small pack containing the gun he had acquired from Sam's cabin. Only a few feet away from the weapon, he reached slowly for it, when the electrified impulses racked his arm.

The clear image of the big cat springing from its perch, outlined by a blue indigo light, engulfed Zak's sight. Instinctively raising his arm in protection, the cat shrieked a ferocious sound upon impact. A familiar crackling noise resounded, then it was silent.

Screaming through the darkness, Sister Julie shouted, "Zak! Oh my God, Zak, what is it, what's happened? Oh my Lord, that horrible squeal."

Zak pulled himself from under the simmering, dead mountain lion. "Sister, try and calm down. It's all over, it's ok now."

Sister Julie held Zak tightly. "But the howl, and the light again…so help me Zak, I thought it was a nightmare. You must have seen it too, the blue glow, and now there's a suffocating odor of burnt fur. Surely you can smell it. You must have seen the strange glare."

Zak took her gently by the shoulders, "Sister, you're not imagining anything. You heard the shriek from the mountain cat that is lying dead by my side. I can only ask that you trust me enough to accept my complete lack of understanding of the blue glow. It's a part of me, in my left arm, and it seems to occur without control. It has a variable intensity to sometimes kill instantly, or just stun. It all began in a terrible electrical storm, where I survived certain death on a mountain top. It sounds like *The Twilight Zone*, I know, but it's the truth, and I'm both blessed and cursed with it."

"You mean like some unknown magnetic force comes upon you at its own will?" she asked.

Zak held his left hand to her face, the blue reflection gone. Visible by flashlight, however, was the long, hideous burn scar running the length of his arm. "Look, Sister, you can see what I see, a grotesque phenomenon, to you as well as myself."

By morning, streams of bright light reflected through the cave entrance revealing an orange sun and a clearing of the snowstorm. Anxiously crawling from their entrapment, Zak and Sister Julie breathed in the cool fresh air at the edge of the mountain.

"Oh, Zak, I can't believe it! Everything is so bright and clear," she exclaimed.

Zak looked at her, his typical half-smile adding more lines to his worn face. "God willing, as you would say, Sister, we'll manage to send a rescue party back to secure Roy's body. For now, let's find out if we can safely descend this ice rock."

CHAPTER 11
THE CRITICAL HOURS

Using whatever remaining rope they had, Zak and Sister Julie tied themselves together, leaving ten to fifteen feet between them.

"Without hooks, pulleys, or proper shoes," Zak urged, "we'll have to rely on each other every step of the way. Whatever happens, if you feel in doubt about any movement going forward, let me know." Sister Julie nodded in silence.

Deep, but melting snow hampered their downward progress. Possible hidden crevices and false snow bridges dictated a careful observance of the slippery terrain. Hours passed before they recognized some diminishing of the ice.

"Sister," Zak yelled through decreasing winds, "I think there are good signs that we may be out of this mess sooner than expected."

As he attempted to navigate a treacherous obstacle of flowing ice and rugged granite, Zak felt the frightening tug of Sister Julie's weight on their short rope. Instinctively, he whirled around to see her bent over form slipping over the mountain edge. All his senses read doom, a fateful occurrence for both he and Sister Julie. There could be no way to prevent this sudden, deathly fall.

Dropping forward on his stomach, his body quickly slid toward the mountain edge, directed by Sister Julie's force. In a final act of desperation, Zak grabbed the taut rope with his left hand. It was as though he had defied the laws of gravity. The pull from Sister Julie's body stopped, and the blue glistening arm halted her fall without difficulty. With his electrified hand clutching the rope as they dangled over the edge, Zak effortlessly pulled her back onto the mountain ledge. He knew the strange, unexplainable energy from his arm had saved their lives.

Zak wondered why Sister Julie had not screamed during this frightening ordeal as he half-carried her crumpled form to a patch of heavy snow. He then realized that Sister Julie had suffered a blackout and remained unconscious. Her jet-black hair rolled aimlessly upon the white snow. After removing a heavy head wrap she had devised to protect herself from the cold and loosening two large collar buttons on her quilted jacket, Zak performed mouth-to-mouth resuscitation. He clutched her frail body and breathed air into her full, oval shaped mouth. The momentary embrace registered a disarming emotion he had never experienced before.

Cradling her, a great relief evolved when a soft whisper of life came from Sister Julie's lips. Zak placed her in a sitting position. "Sister, Sister, are you all right, can you hear me?"

Faintly, she replied, "Yes, Zak, I'm so sorry, I don't know what happened. Maybe my head injury is worse than I thought. I still have that enormous headache, which frankly has been with me since the plane accident. I should have mentioned it, but I thought it would eventually subside."

"We can't stay here under these conditions," Zak insisted, "I think it best that I assist you and we proceed slowly. We have no other choice, Sister, I—"

"—Zak, I understand, let's go on and do what me must."

Two days had passed before a five-man search party had reached the snow level of Sherman Mountain. Their search report told of a small Cessna airplane, presumed to be down in the treacherous, icy mountain crevasses. Incomplete details also included that two or three people were possibly aboard the fateful aircraft.

The story of a flickering blue light sighted near the summit was dismissed as a delusion of two champagne drinking pilots from Las Vegas.

Carrying emergency stretchers and other rescue equipment, the search team began a precarious climb into the relentless snowstorm. Words of instructions were shared from various individuals as they proceeded into the blinding snow wall.

One of the team members shouted, "Hey, hold it, I think I see an image of something coming toward us. I don't know if it's walking or crawling, but it's coming into focus."

Before them approached a tall, ghostly-white figure carrying a limp, bedraggled body. Zak's completely void face behind his heavily iced ski hood presented a ghostly aberration.

"I hope you guys are for real, because I don't think I can carry this injured woman any further," Zak gasped, falling to his knees.

CHAPTER 12
TAKING TO THE ROAD
AGAIN

Coffee stains and a few sweet rolls remained in a carboard box where the rescue team had indulged their appetites. Their conversations regarding the Sherman Mountain incident took on theatrical proportions.

"Man, this big, scary guy comes out of the blinding storm like the Abominable Snowman," one uniformed rescuer exclaimed.

"Yeah," said another, and no telling how long he's been carrying this woman, a nun no less."

"She's in bad shape, with multiple head injuries, and in fact, they're preparing her for surgery," the only female member added. "The guy's doing remarkably well, considering the incredible ordeal. They have him in the conference room now answering questions. Imagine, this character has a hang up about removing that heavy, hooded ski jacket. Examining him hasn't been easy."

"Takes all kinds, Lisa," the team leader asserted as he poured coffee from the hospital percolator. "Weird or not, if my gut feeling is correct, this guy performed a superhuman feat."

The hospital conference room contained a small oval table with six chairs surrounding its perimeter. The chief surgeon and the hospital administrator, Mr. Kurtz, sat across from Zak and began questioning him.

"Mr... ah, I understand we do not know your last name, and that you prefer just to be called Zak; so, for now, I'll accommodate. Zak, have we been rightly informed, that you and Sister Julie were proceeding to St. James Hospital in Twin Falls by plane when severe turbulence forced your plane down?"

Zak paused, then turned his head slowly to face his interrogator. "Our pilot, named Roy, decided to engage the emergency procedure, and rightly so. The ice storm came upon us instantly, forcing a crash landing before a possible mid-air break up."

My Kurtz continued, "Three days ago, the police reported a distress call from another private plane flying at night near Sherman Mountain. The pilot, along with a passenger, spotted—or thought they spotted—an unidentified blue signal or electrical arch coming from the interior of the mountain. Mr. Zak, did you see any such phenomenon, or can you offer any explanation?"

A grim smile crossed Zak's veiled face. "The only color I recall, Mr. Kurtz, is white—snow white. Now, if possible, I would like to see Sister Julie as soon as she's able."

"If necessary, you'll be able to say a few words before we take her into surgery," the doctor replied, "but in the meantime, Zak, if you could avail yourself to the Sheriff and his staff, they would like to ask a few required questions. They should be here in ten minutes or so."

Zak looked nervously at the big white clock on the wall, then back at Mr. Kurtz and the quiet head surgeon. "Sure, Mr. Kurtz, anything I can do to help the authorities."

Finally, the surgeon, Dr. O'Donohue, spoke. "I'll take good care of the sister, Zak, you can be sure of that."

Both the administrator and the physician rose from their chairs, smiled, and walked from the conference room. Sitting alone, his hands folded on the table, Zak pondered his risky position. He went to the conference room door and opened it slightly to observe two uniformed police officers talking to the hospital staff. Quickly moving to the back of the room, Zak opened a sliding glass patio door leading to a fire escape.

He thought sadly of Sister Julie and the fact that he may never see her again, and then adeptly stepping to the black grating, he scampered down three flights of the metallic stairway. "Ok, pal, hold it right there—freeze mister!" a voice from a nearby doorway barked. A uniformed police officer approached, branding a gun and a pair of handcuffs. "I don't know what your big hurry is, buddy, but just turn around, put your hands behind your back, and we'll talk about it," he ordered.

Zak turned his back toward the trooper, his head bowed. "I'm sorry about this officer, but do me and yourself a favor, and please don't put those cuffs on me. I can't explain it now, but I have an affliction…I mean, it's dangerous when encountering metal."

"Sure it is, mister, and I'm really Superman, so nothing can hurt me," the officer growled, slapping the handcuffs solidly to Zak's wrist.

An electrical *bang* could be heard throughout the causeway. The trooper stiffened, groaned a chocking noise, then curled to the ground. A small whirl of smoke surrounded his prostrate body. Zak stood still, with only one handcuff secured to his wrist. The other dangled, the shiny metal having turned a crusty black color. His instincts bolted him down a narrow alley and to a small gateway leading to the hospital parking lot; the familiar burnt flesh odor filled the air.

As he surveyed the parking lot, he noticed several police officers crowding around two squad cars. At a distance, two men manned a single hospital ramp. They were loading a medium-sized truck with heavy equipment. The truck driver appeared to be asleep in the cab, his head protruding partly out the driver window.

The sound of the truck's big rear doors slamming shut echoed, and a harsh voice yelled, "Time to come to life, Mozart, you're late again, so get the heck out of here, big daddy." The driver jolted from his slumber and instantly started the motor.

He then turned to look back at his counterparts. "You bums sure know how to hurt a guy. There I was, on a South Sea Island beach with Miss America," he groaned.

The truck chugged forward in slow motion, then the engine caught and smoothly moved the vehicle toward Zak's position. With cat-like reflexes, Zak crouched to a low-profile and moved stealthily toward the passenger side of the truck. Grabbing the door handle, he opened it, and maneuvered to sit next to the startled driver.

"Sorry, pal," Zak murmured, "but I'm in need of a quick lift like you wouldn't believe."

The wide-eyed driver calmly replied, "Never argue with a desperate man, my momma done told me." He proceeded to turn the large steering wheel, swinging the truck down a slight incline and through an exit ramp to the main highway.

Zak's benefactor, a burly black man whose frame seemed to be stuffed between the seat and the steering wheel, stared at Zak with a wry grin. "You look more like the grim reaper than someone on the run, mister. I suppose that bunch of cops hanging around the hospital has a lot to do with it. Anyway, I can offer you a ride, but if you're fixin' for money, you've hit the bottom of the barrel here."

"Have no fear, Mozart—I heard your friends call you that—I'm only interested in distancing myself from the parking lot. And don't let my hood bother you; it's just to cover up an ugly face."

An even wider smile came to Mozart's face as he pushed the truck accelerator to the floor.

"They call me Mozart because I write music, but my real name is Morris; that's right, a music writing truck driver. Nothing published yet, just a hundred crazy ditties only I know and sing while I'm on the road.

Zak chuckled. "Sounds good to me, Mozart. You might be the next trucker to compose another "On the Road Again." The two strangers both smiled.

The white, unmarked hospital truck cruised at a fast speed on the darkening highway. Looking straight ahead at the road and beginning to feel more at ease, Mozart spoke to Zak.

"I usually take a slight detour to visit my girlfriend, Sarah, at a small diner if it doesn't bother you, Mr.—"

"—Just call me Zak, and do whatever it is you do, Mo. I just want to get out of here."

"Great, she'll be surprised; I never stop by on Mondays," Mozart replied, wheeling the truck around a tight curve and down an incline.

They soon entered the small town of Jolson, where a scattering of run-down shacks and businesses revealed an obvious struggle with poverty.

"This town is mostly black, mister," quipped Mo, "but if it suits you, you're about to taste the finest homemade cheeseburgers in America. They should be called 'Sarah Burgers.'

Zak grinned. "Mo, the way your 300 pounds fills up that driver's seat, I think you've been indulging in more of Sarah's specialties than you admit to." Again, they both chuckled.

After parking the truck in a sandy area next to an old, but well-kept storefront, they proceeded up a long stairway attached to the side of the building. Mozart used a key and opened the paint-chipped door.

Immediately upon entering, the unmistakable sound of a man and woman's muffled voices could be heard. Their vocal expressions were those of obvious intimate pleasure. Zak noticed the concerned look on Mo's face. His heavy-set frame was frozen in its tracks in the short hallway.

He gripped Mo by the arm. "Mo, whatever you think, whatever this means, we have no right to impose on your friend Sarah like this. Stay calm, stay cool, and we'll leave to announce ourselves later. I know what you're thinking, Mo, and I can't blame you, but out of respect for her, shouldn't we leave?" Zak could see the inner rage in the rippling veins of Mo's neck.

Surprisingly, a tall, gaunt black man—partly covered with a blanket and wielding a switch-blade—scrambled into the hallway.

"Well, if it ain't the fattest man in the county, Mo Mo the musical moron from New Orleans."

The obviously drunk figure swayed recklessly against the hallway walls. Then, swinging his knife wildly, he sprang at Mo, jabbing the menacing blade into Mo's shoulder. Oblivious to the blow, Mo pulled the knife from his own body and shoved it against the neck of his adversary, pinning him in a death lock against the wall. Zak clamored up the back of Mo's giant body and grasped his wrist, desperately trying to pull the knife away.

Zak hooked his other arm around Mo's neck in a stranglehold. "Mo, you kill this creep, and everything you hope for goes out the window; believe me, he ain't worth it," he yelled.

When he reached the bedroom, he found a beautiful nude girl cowering in uncontrollable hysteria behind a torn sheet. She was not Sarah, but a friend of hers who had often used the apartment periodically.

"Who the heck are you?" Mo shouted, but in her trauma, the young woman could only scream.

Mo whirled around at the sight of a blue light streaming through the narrow hallway, silhouetting the skinny character raising his switchblade over Zak.

"Behind you!" screamed Mo.

Zak turned, raising his electrified arm in protection. Engulfed in a blinding flash, Mo instinctively fell to the floor. Even the few lights in the upstairs room went out.

Only the continuous crying of the young girl could be heard in the blackness. Mo rose slowly to his knees when he saw the eerie blue glow fading in the tunnel-like hallway.

TAKING TO THE ROAD AGAIN

Crawling on his hands and knees, Mo spoke. "Zak, Zak, are you ok? What happened? What's causing the neon light, man?" Then, all went into total darkness.

"Mo, this is Zak—I'm alright, but our druggy friend is not doing too well. I'll go into the basement and see if we haven't blown a fuse. If the lights go on, take a look at this guy; I think he could be in bad shape."

Mo could hear Zak shuffle, then his footsteps running down the outside stairs. He leaned against the wall, completely perplexed in the silent blackness. A strange odor filled his nostrils.

The lights blinked on momentarily, and Mo could see a blanket-covered body curled in a heap. As he quickly examined their attacker, he observed a wide burn scar covering the entire length of his lifeless body.

Zak re-entered the apartment, out of breath. "Mo, what's with the weirdo, how is he?"

"He's dead, man, I mean stone cold dead. And I don't know about you, but I smell something burning, and look at the horrible burn on this nut."

Zak examined the body. "Let's hope the girl stops crying so you and I can get the heck out of here."

After backing the hospital truck from the grassy area and rolling out onto the highway, Zak and Mo remained silent for many miles before Mo spoke.

"Zak, did you see the strange blue light in the hallway, or am I crazy?"

"I did, Mo, and I do know of it. For now, I must ask that you trust me until I can be sure, ok?"

Mo just looked at Zak without commenting.

Driving through the night, Mo shook his sleeping passenger. "Zak, Zak, wake up, friend. The sun is rising over the mountains, and I think we could both use some rest. There's a small group of cabins coming up to the right."

They entered a narrow driveway leading to a scattering of six unique cabins, and Mo pulled the truck to a stop.

Zak peered lazily from the passenger seat. "This place looks like the Garden of Eden in the middle of the desert," he commented.

"I come here often," Mo replied, "a man bigger than me, named Tiny, runs this place."

"Mighty Mo," came a voice from behind a row of cacti decorating the reception office. An extremely rotund gentleman waddled toward their vehicle.

"Mighty Mo, the Music Man," their greeter repeated, "didn't expect you back so soon, Mozart. Who's your partner?

Mo stepped down from the cab and shook the hand of their friendly host. "Tiny, it's good to see you, and my friend here is Zak. How's everything going at the Oasis?"

"Plenty to drink, Mo, if you know what I mean. It's nice to meet you, Zak," Tiny waved, smiling.

After a cordial exchange of conversation, the weary travelers secured comfortable lodging. The owner, Tiny Beecham, had designed and labored long to maintain a greenhouse-like atmosphere within his unique cottage respite. Upon retiring to their small rooms, Mo fell immediately into a deep sleep. Even the unexpected ringing of the doorbell failed to wake him.

Zak rose from his bed and quickly entered the compact living room. After hesitating for a moment, he opened the door. "Hello?"

"Yes, it's me, Tiny. I'm sorry to bother you guys again, but something just dawned upon me, and you might want to tell Mo. Just before you two arrived, three gentlemen and a young lady drove into my establishment. They were inquiring about a friend of theirs…at least that's what they said.

"I recall now that their description of this friend detailed a person wearing a dark blue hood, or ski jacket, as they put it. I just remembered your appearance and figured you might like to know. Oh, and they gave me a blue gambling chip from Vegas. One guy said if I ever get to the strip, this chip will come in handy. Next thing I knew, they drove away in the biggest limousine in this state."

"Thanks, Tiny," Zak replied. Stunned, he closed the door and walked back into the bedroom, his thoughts rambling.

Hard to believe they are still looking for me. How could the Maniatis family have traced me to this place? He wondered.

Laying back across the bed, Zak rubbed his tired eyes and pulled back the cumbersome hood where heavy scars reflected. He succumbed to exhaustion into a grateful sleep.

Later that night, a loud moan startled Zak, causing him to sit up stiffly in the bed. When the moan came again, he leapt from the covers and rushed into Mo's room. Zak saw his big body wrenching from obvious pain.

"Mo, Mo, what is it, man? What's happening?"

Mo turned over in a severe twisting motion and could barely respond. "It's my dang heart again, I left my pills in—" his words stopped.

"My God, man, a heart attack," came Zak's panicked voice.

After opening Mo's collar and placing pillows under his head, Zak felt for a pulse.

"Nothing, and I think he's stopped breathing. Mo, pal, can you hear me? I'm going to give you mouth-to-mouth resuscitation…hang in there, big fella."

Zak began applying the cardiopulmonary resuscitation procedure, pausing at intervals to wait for a response from the man who had so warmly befriended him.

Getting no response from the CPR treatment, Zak immediately switched to pressing both of his hands to Mo's chest. Still, no visible signs of consciousness occurred.

"Come on, Mo, you're too tough to let this thing do you in." With time becoming a critical factor, Zak's urgings and hand pounding intensified.

"Oh No," Zak cried as he felt the customary tremor enter his left arm, followed by a gradual fluorescent blue glow lighting the dark bedroom.

Zak removed his left arm from Mo's body and held it up close to his own face. "What a time for you to…wait a minute, I wonder if it could be possible to…" His eyes looked hypnotically at the bluish-green iridescent arm.

Hesitantly, Zak made a fist and placed his electrified hand over Mo's body. Slowly but firmly, he barely tapped the middle chest area. Big Mo's body erupted from the bed, and a slight sound came from him. Zak lightly pounded again, and a shock created the same knee-jerk response.

Zak repeated the tapping until Mo eventually turned his head and spoke. "What's with the big light? What's happening, Zak? Where am I?"

Zak smiled in relief, his illuminated, pulsating arm subsiding. He pulled the covers up and over Mo's form.

"Mo, forget the light, it's great to see your bright face. Try to relax, partner, and get some sleep. You suffered a heart attack and had me worried for a while, big guy. Right now, I can't figure out how or what happened myself, but you're ok, and that's all that counts," he assured him. "You mentioned some pills—if you have some, where are they?"

With eyes closed, Mo responded, "In the truck's glove compartment, and thanks."

Locating the small bottle of prescription pills, Zak decided to move the big truck to an area in the rear of the cabin compound. After delivering the medication to Mo, he walked back to his billet and set an alarm clock for a three-hour sleep, knowing their stay could not be longer.

Awaking Mo in the early evening, Zak told him of a need for urgency. "Mo, without a long story, please take my word for it; we must leave this watering hole now. We need to get you to a doctor. I'll get the truck and help you into it."

His weak comrade simply nodded affirmatively.

Zak hurriedly stepped from the cottage and started to jog to where he had parked the truck. An explosion brought him swiftly to a prone position on the scrub grass. Looking up from his hood, Zak could see the cabin where he had parked the truck had exploded into an instant inferno.

"Christ!" he shouted, jumping to his feet. He ran to the small driveway adjacent to the burning cottage and leapt into the truck cab, quickly backing it away from the fire.

Driving wildly toward his cottage, Tiny, the owner of the cottages appeared in the headlights, frantically waving his arms.

Zak skid the truck to a halt and Tiny jumped on the driver's side running board. "Zak! My God, something or someone has blown up a rear area unit," he yelled, "I've called the firehouse! Thankfully, the cottage is empty. Lord in Heaven, nothing like this has ever happened here before! Look at that crazy fireball; the whole thing is incinerated! What do you make of it?"

CHAPTER 12

"Tiny, by the time the fire truck gets here, Mo and I will be gone. I wish I could be sure of what caused the explosion," Zak paused, "but whatever, there isn't anything we can do to help. Mo is sick. And I've got to get him medical assistance immediately."

Tiny jumped from the truck as Zak shifted into low gear. The vehicle rumbled toward the cottage where Mozart waited.

Tiny's silhouette stood out against the bright orange and red inferno as Zak pulled away in the truck with Mo resting in the passenger seat.

Complete darkness enveloped the desert, with the lone headlight beams revealing the hospital vehicle's high rate of speed. Mo's head jostled against a small pillow Zak had acquired from the cottage.

"Zak, if that blaze had any connection with you and why you're avoiding certain people, something tells me this is going to be a trip to remember," Mo muttered quietly.

Zak drove persistently and looked forward, a steely expression lining his face. "Right now, my biggest concern is about your health, big guy, but I promise I'll explain things to you later."

TAKING TO THE ROAD AGAIN

Driving on through the night, Zak squinted at the first rays of the Arizona sun splashing against the windshield. Mo had taken more of his heart pills and attempted to convince Zak that his condition, although worrisome, was not life-threatening.

"Ok, Mozart, I'll go along with your miracle pill story," Zak urged, "but I still think we should have a doctor look at you."

He swung the big steering wheel to navigate a sharp turn, throwing Mo away from his comfortable pillow.

"Hey, brother, a man could suffer a fatal heart attack just from your driving; this ain't no Ferrari—uh oh, Zak, do you see in your side view mirror what I see?"

Turning his head sharply, Zak peered into the oversized mirror. "As if anything more could go wrong… It looks like the State Police."

CHAPTER 13
THE DESERT ORDEAL

After watching the revolving red light splash its beams against the side view mirror, Zak slowly pulled the truck off the road and onto a dusty area. Concentrating on the mirror, he continued to watch as a short, uniformed trooper approached.

Wearing sunglasses above a heavy mustache, the officer smiled and spoke in a heavy Latino accent. "Hey, hombre, what's the big hurry for such a large truck so early in the morning?"

"Sorry, officer," Zak answered, "I have a very sick patient with me, and I'm hoping to find a doctor in the next town."

The officer, still smiling, opened the truck door, giving him a better view of Mo's resting position. "Si, I think your compadre looks a little under the weather. Maybe if you'd like, we can offer some help?"

Before Zak could answer, the trooper walked back to the squad car to get assistance.

Zak looked back at Mo. "That's kind of strange, don't you think, Mo? Look through your mirror; there are three other officers in the patrol car."

Within seconds, two officers stood on each side of the truck. The one who had previously approached spoke again. "Hombre, we have been waiting for you for such a long time. Looks like you got side-tracked somewhere along the way, huh? Our information said that only one driver would be in this truck and would arrive here many hours ago."

Mo leaned over. "Ok, trooper—if you are a trooper— what the heck is this all about? And your fellow officers, why aren't they saying anything? Or is it because they can't speak English?"

"Señor, you are very perceptive," the smiling officer remarked, "perhaps we have taken advantage of you with our shiny badges and flashing lights."

Drawing a police special revolver from his holster, he continued. "You see, amigo, we know of the important medical equipment you carry on this plain white truck. It is the kind of scientific machinery that many of my country's hospitals are desperate for."

"Yeah, and which a lot of people will pay big money for," bristled Mo.

The tall, masquerading officer's smile broadened even further, displaying his bright white teeth. "Amigo, your country has so much money piled from coast to coast, no one will miss one small truckload lost in the desert. Besides, some wealthy American insurance company will pay the bill for all of this. ¿Si?"

With a hand instruction from their leader, the other uniformed men drew their guns.

The tall imposter, waving the revolver, continued. "Caballeros, I ask that you both step from the truck and find more comfort in our new patrol car."

Zak helped Mo, and they carefully stepped from the truck, proceeded toward the state police car, and entered the back seat. The "officer" and a companion followed, taking the front seats while the two other captors manned the truck.

Taking the driver's seat of the patrol car, the leader pointed his gun. "Amigos, we will have to travel a short distance to a small arroyo. If you relax, I hope it will not be necessary to tie you up. ¿Comprendo?"

While they followed the hospital truck, the police radio intermittently blared out calls of four missing state police officers and two patrol cars. The messages detailed a report of an all-points bulletin on the lookout for suspected illegal immigrants within the surrounding area.

The police radio concluded the suspects were armed and dangerous.

"Amigos," the leader chided, "how do you like the way the radio speaks of us in such bad ways? We are only doing the humanitarian thing for the health and welfare of those in our country. Our people do not know much about laser beams, or CAT scans, or MRIs. This truckload will be a blessing from heaven for so many thousands of people in need."

"Yeah," snapped Mo, "providing somebody pays you for the blessing, eh?"

The man looked down as he spoke. "Señor, I am like your famous Robin Hood who took from the rich and gave to the poor. The only difference is, I do ask for a show of appreciation, which we call *muchos centavos*." The man and his companion laughed.

The two vehicles proceeded off the roadway, both engines straining over the sandy surface. Shortly, they approached an incline where the headlights revealed a small arroyo. In the center of the desert pocket, two poorly built lean-to sheds stood partly covered by blowing sand. Alongside both structures, the smoldering of a campfire remained. Close by, a three-quarter ton army truck appeared mired in a deep sand gully.

Coming to a halt, all occupants stepped from the vehicle while the leader shouted orders to his subordinates. Zak and Mo were instructed to sit alongside the ashes while one captor attempted to relight the campfire.

Strangely, two of the armed captors appeared to stay at a distance from the rest of the group.

Mo whispered to Zak, "I wonder what's with the two banditos who want to be left alone."

Zak only looked up, the first glows of the fire casting an eerie flicker of light across his jagged face.

The leader approached, his perennial smile preempting his words. "Hombres, the desert can be so cold at night, especially in this arroyo. We will see that a good fire keeps us all comfortable."

Then, his smile diminished, and he leaned over directly in front of Zak. "Señor, I do not wish any disrespect, but it seems my compadres have some childish ideas of you."

Zak remained mute and continued his stare.

Looking at Zak, he shook his head. "Señor, you must understand that my friends are from a small town in Chile called Lasto Minicos, where there is much superstition." He hesitated, "Please accept my apology on their behalf. It seems they have a name for you; you are

'The Ghost Man.' They will not join us unless you show your face, amigo."

Zak looked slowly toward the two uniformed figures standing at a distance in the semi-darkness. He then looked up.

"Robin Hood, tell your partners that I'm just a man, and if they come to the campfire, I'll remove my hood."

The leader stood and smiled again. "Gracious señor, I have tried to tell them just that, but they must see for themselves."

He walked toward his friends, shouting in Spanish, and waving his arms. All watched the two huddled figures walk clumsily over to the campfire, their fearful eyes riveted on Zak.

Sitting opposite the fire from Zak, the two fretful Chileans gawked as Zak pulled back his heavy, dark hood. Colorful reflections from the fire formed a grotesque image of his disfigured face, and a gasp could be heard from one anxious bandito.

The man who called himself Robin Hood broke the tension with berating words in Spanish. "Pablo, Carlos, I hope you are satisfied. It is time to get our work done now, with no more delays! Bring the tortillas and beans; we will cook some food for the long night."

Apparently still threatened, the two Chileans did not sit at the campfire, but walked slowly behind a nearby lean-to.

Robin Hood made frequent calls on his portable phone without making any contacts. The stressful night continued, with a flaming campfire and occasional shrills of desert creatures. Unable to sleep, Zak and Mo watched as their captors mulled around in anxious concern over their inability to make phone communications.

A piercing ring of the portable phone shrilled the night air, followed by the shuffling of Robin Hood to answer the call.

"Si, si Señor," he stammered.

The brief conversation brought a sense of relief to the band of imposters.

Robin Hood quickly walked over to Zak's sleeping form. "Señor, I am sorry to disturb you and your friend, but it is time to proceed with our important journey. We do have a task that must be taken care of before we leave, and we insist that you both help."

An abrupt reply from a long-silenced Mo revealed his frustration. "What do you want from us? We're your prisoners, and right now our concern is getting out of this thing alive."

A momentary silence added to the obvious friction.

"Señor," he said, sitting down on a rock next to Mozart. "We ask only that you give us a hand and use some of your muscle to assist us in pulling our disabled truck from the ditch. We will need to transfer the medical equipment into this army truck, and as you can see, our plans went slightly off track."

"In our haste, my amigo miscalculated the severe incline and drove into the ditch. If you look further, we have already attached a cable where the four of us could not remove the truck. Maybe two more large-sized hombres like you two could make it possible."

Zak rose from his position and began to walk toward the tilted truck. "I know you're hurting, Mo, but we have little choice. And besides, we should get these guys out of here as fast as we can."

Mo followed him, along with the entire group, although the two reluctant Chileans walked around and away from 'The Ghost Man.'

Again, Robin Hood began shouting instructions in Spanish to his followers. Zak and Mo took a position at the end of the long cable, while the leader slid down into the sandy ditch, placing himself at the front of the army truck.

"When I signal, señors, everybody pull!" he yelled.

With five men holding the cable taut, Zak experienced the mystical tremor in his left arm. He turned to Mo, who stood behind him.

"Mo, when I tell you, let go of the cable, and don't argue," he urged.

Robin Hood began to push and gave the signal for the others to pull. Immediately, the truck began to level off as it moved slowly from the ditch.

Zak whispered, "Mo, let go," and a blinding streak of white, green, and blue electricity burrowed through the steel cable, hitting the truck in a burst of electromagnetic fire. Hideous screams could be heard, followed by the crashing of the truck back to the bottom of the sand gully.

Mo, laying on his back, looked in disbelief at a smoking carnage of prostrate bodies, all lined up alongside the smoldering cable. Only Zak stood amidst the human rubble.

He frantically ran to Mo's aid. "Mo, are you ok, have you been burned at all?"

Mo, unable to talk, just looked, as though paralyzed.

"Mo, are you ok, can you hear me?" Zak repeated.

Mo, barely audible, replied, "I don't believe what I saw."

Their attention quickly diverted to a groan from behind the fallen truck. "It's Robin Hood," Zak shouted, running down the small embankment.

Pinned beneath the front structure of the army truck, Robin Hood's smoking body moved in agony.

"Robin Hood, you're alive, try not to move, we'll get help, we—"

Robin Hood interrupted, his voice only a whisper, "Pablo, Carlos, they were right, you are a 'Ghost Man,'" his eyed closed.

While he kneeled over the dying man, Zak painfully turned to Mo.

"Mo, I know this incredible blood bath makes no sense, and perhaps your impulse is to remain and try to understand this puzzle. But we can no longer help these people. There is nothing we can do; we must leave this place now. I promised to tell you of my terrible dilemma, it will explain a lot. Right now, grab the portable phone, and let's get ourselves out of here."

CHAPTER 14
ESCAPE TO NOWHERE

The pair traveled all through the night and into the next day. Mo, seated in the passenger side of the hospital truck, spoke slowly.

"Zak, your story sounds more like a nightmare than anything real. It's as though some dark, unearthly magnetic force has possessed your body. There's no explanation; however, certainly the high-tension wires, along with the devastating electrical storm you experienced, created the phenomenon. You're like a walking lightning bolt; it's too much to comprehend."

"Tell me about it," winced Zak, "I can only hope that as sudden as it came, it may leave me the same way."

A news report from the truck radio told of an unpredictable electrical storm that had electrocuted four illegal immigrants, the same group previously sought by police. Zak nodded in relief, as the desert storm mentioned had probably wiped out all traces of their tire tracks leaving the arroyo.

Going without sleep for long periods had become a way of life for Zak and he felt that fatigue now. Fighting to concentrate on his driving, he addressed Mo.

"Mo, if you're being honest about how the heart pills have stabilized your condition, I'm going to part company real soon. Roy's Old Crow Way Station—and I hope my repaired Pontiac—is just up the road. I'm holding you to your promise to stop for medical assistance at the first town before delivering the medical supplies."

Mo smiled through his now stubbly, graying beard. "It's been a *Twilight Zone* experience, Zak, and I promise to write you into my next Mozart ditty. My heart is fine, but I'll keep the promise; I'll see a doctor as soon as possible."

Then it appeared, covered in dust, and still looking abandoned, the dilapidated Old Crow Way Station. Pulling the truck barely under the tilted canopy, Zak stepped from the cab.

"Just give me a minute, Mozart, and if my car is operable, you can be on your way."

As he opened the station door, he was surprised to see a man in coveralls sitting at Roy's desk.

"I'm Luke, and I bet you're Zak," the attendant said. "Roy left me a note telling me to fix the GTO and to give it to the man who hides his face with a hood. Ain't many people wearing a hood in this desert country, Zak. Roy said only you would have the only duplicate key and the combination to the safe."

Zak turned back to wave off Mo. "Maybe we'll meet again, Mozart; drive carefully and keep that promise." He could see Mo wave and watched as the white truck pulled away.

"Luke," he held out his hand, dangling two keys, "I need to transfer some personal belongings from the safe to my car. If you have repaired the engine, I'll pay the bill and be out of your hair in ten minutes."

Luke walked toward the cleaned-up Pontiac GTO. "She's like new, Zak, and if you're not too upset, I took it for a rip-roaring cruise to prove it."

After removing the two heavy bags of gold from the safe and placing them in the car trunk, Zak handed Luke a generous amount of money. "Luke, I think this should be enough to cover my bill."

Stepping into the green convertible while Luke opened the shabby garage door, Zak gave a thumbs up signal as the canvas top folded down. A rumble from the high-performance engine carried him swiftly onto the seemingly endless desert highway.

Warm desert air streamed across his face, again pushing the ski hood back, and Zak's mind contemplated the long journey ahead. He pushed the accelerator to the floor and decided to cross as many states as possible, as quickly as possible.

Covering a two-state distance in a Herculean effort, the once sparkling green GTO—now coated in dark-reddish dust—moved slowly into a South Dakota car wash. As Zak watched the swirly, soapy water blur the windshield, his thoughts turned to notions of hope. To his relief, his electrified arm had not reappeared during the long haul.

"Maybe I've beaten this thing; it's been a long time now," he murmured, fighting to stay awake.

"Hey mister, mister, wake up," shouted the car wash attendant, as he knocked on the driver window. The Pontiac had stopped at the end of the wash cycle, and without continuing, the treadmill mechanism automatically ceased.

The attendant opened the car door. "Hey, mister, sorry to bother you, but this is the first time a customer has fallen asleep in our car wash."

Zak shook his head, "Sorry pal, I guess I've been driving too long."

"No problem," replied the worker, "why don't you get some shut eye at the forest preserve lot just across the road."

"Thanks," Zak nodded and handed the attendant a few crumpled bills.

Experiencing a dizzy sensation, he drove the convertible into the lush preserve where a small black-top parking area offered rest.

After a few restful minutes, a blinding light as bright as the sun itself engulfed his senses, and Zak feared another chilling nightmare was about overtake him.

A forceful voice broke the frightful glare. "Wake up, buddy, we have to close this lot at eleven o'clock." The stern face of a uniformed police officer came into focus. He pulled the flashlight away and continued, "You've been sleeping a long-time buddy, according to Tom at the car wash."

Zak carefully leaned back in the driver's seat. "Sorry officer, guess I shouldn't have tried to drive from Nevada non-stop."

The officer looked back at his flashing squad car, then leaned on the Pontiac door frame. "Well, stranger, anyone who drives a marathon like that should be entitled to sleep until daylight. I'll have to put up the chain gate, but I'm going to let you stay here until tomorrow. I drove an eighteen-wheeler myself not too long ago, so I know what sleep deprivation can do to a man; see you in the morning."

Zak watched as the policeman drove his official car to the entrance gate, pulled and locked a single chain across the driveway. Complete darkness enveloped him again and he fell across the front seat, exhausted. He wondered if this too was not a dream.

A beautiful sound of birds chirping wildly through a patch of small berry trees brought Zak up to a sitting position. A low ground mist mingled through the morning break and a fresh dew sprinkled atop a field of manicured grass. Surveying the beautiful preserve surroundings, he noticed a prepared jogging path. It had been a long time since he enjoyed one of his favorite pastimes—running. He figured, why not?

Jogging at a controlled speed, Zak began to feel a rekindled spirit. As he passed close to a line of underbrush and colorfully draped trees, he took deep breaths of exhilaration. Some of the trees formed a tunnel path reaching across and overhead.

Increasing his running gate through the canopied roof of branches and leaves, Zak relished an easy stride. The path twisted and curved a scenic expanse along the wood-chipped track. He reached a fork in the course and slowed before choosing the left direction. Immediately, he came to a grass field opening, where a group of children were sitting atop a picnic bench. Not wanting to alarm them, Zak stopped to walk. However, two of the children began to run toward him. Stopping to await their arrival, he realized their frantic cries.

"Mister, mister, it's Miss Taylor, Miss Taylor, they've taken her...they've gone into the woods!" shouted one of the small boys.

"Hold it, settle down," Zak urged, holding his hands out to stop their frenzy. "Miss Taylor, the woods, what happened? Slow down," he pleaded.

Out of breath, the taller of the two boys told a harrowing story of an abduction of their schoolteacher by two scary men. The children, part of a school field trip, were enjoying a picnic with their teacher when the terrifying incident happened.

"Which way did they take her?" Zak asked. Both boys pointed at the very path Zak had come from. Running back to the direction he had covered, Zak yelled, "You boys go back on the bench and watch out for the others. I'm going to count on you; I'll be back real soon."

As he again reached the fork in the jogging path, he realized the abductors must have taken the other direction from which he took. Running at top speed, he heard what sounded like loud rock music. He stopped momentarily as he realized the direction of the music came from off the path. Turning, he attempted to plow through the heavy underbrush, following the wailing staccato sound of a boom box.

Tripping over a twisted array of surface rocks, Zak tumbled to the ground. As he instinctively grabbed onto a rotting log, the foreboding bluish glow of his arm outlined the forest floor. Leaping to his feet and using his electrified limb as a battering ram, Zak burrowed through small trees and entangled brush.

He reached a small clearing and saw a woman, partially clothed, lying on the ground screaming and flailing her hands. A bearded, slovenly dressed man stood over her, attempting to grab her hands. Another jeering character held a small chain and a large, blaring portable radio over his own head, threatening to silence her. They both whirled around upon hearing the foraging of Zak's intrusion.

The man with the chain rushed at Zak and swung his heavy weapon at Zak's head. But the chain struck Zak's raised electric arm with a *crack* sound, flinging the culprit to the ground in a burning heap. Now holding the illuminated chain himself, Zak turned on the second figure who decided to run. Chasing him, Zak brought the blue, glistening chain down on the tormentor's back. A bolt of electricity flashed, burying the bearded abuser into deep grass. Both vagabonds' bodies lay lifeless in a smoking, double circle of grass.

Dropping the chain as his glowing arm began to subside, Zak walked back to the delirious woman who was screaming uncontrollably. He knelt to console her when she fell into an unconscious state. Carefully, he replaced her clothes and carried her back to the picnic area where the children ran to him, screaming their concern.

"She's okay," assured Zak, "someone bring me that jug of water," he shouted.

Laying out blankets and a makeshift pillow to comfort their stricken teacher, the children assisted Zak in bringing her back to consciousness. She began to cry sobs of thankfulness.

Zak spoke to the children. "Kids, you've done a great job, and your teacher is going to be all right. I see the school bus is pulling into the parking lot to the west. You, the boy with the blonde hair, what's your name?"

"Joseph," the still shaken youngster replied.

Zak smiled. "Well, Joe, I want you to run to the bus and inform the other teachers of our problem. Tell them

Miss Taylor is ok, but we need a stretcher if they have one."

The gangly nine-year-old said nothing but turned and ran quickly toward the yellow bus.

A crowd of concerned associates soon arrived to assist the injured teacher. Within minutes, they carried her to a school bus to be taken to a nearby hospital. Her sporadic sobbing could be heard as the bus moved swiftly from the parking lot.

Zak's presence was lost in the overall traumatic atmosphere of crying children and shouting adults. He casually walked back toward the jogging path when the young boy named Joseph ran up to him.

"Hey Mister," he shouted, "whatever happened to the two bad men?"

"I'm counting on you again, Joseph, to tell the authorities to follow that forest jogging path leading to the right, not the left," Zak pointed. "Tell them to take the newly made path of broken trees leading to a burned patch of grass."

Joseph quizzically smiled. "Ok," he answered, then waved cautiously before running back toward the parking lot.

On board the bus, the traumatized teacher, Miss Taylor, told a semi-coherent story of her shocking experience. The puzzled looks of her fellow teachers revealed thoughts of possible hallucinations. Her account of a mysterious hooded benefactor—whose face she never saw—emerging from the woods brought raised eyebrows.

ESCAPE TO NOWHERE

CHAPTER 15
HONORING A PROMISE

Driving just outside Sioux Falls, South Dakota, only ten miles from the Minnesota border, Zak felt content that he would soon complete the lengthy journey. As he approached the designated town of Wayzata, the weather in Minnesota took on an unusually warm, colorful day.

He stopped at a quaint lake side café adjoined by piers, where a small fleet of cabin cruisers were moored, and read the final directions on Sam Rooney's crumpled note. According to those instructions, Zak calculated he could not be more than fifteen minutes away from Sam's daughter's place.

"May I help you, sir?" came the voice of a young, uniformed waitress.

"Just coffee, please," Zak replied, "oh, and do you happen to know where the Tamara home is?"

"I don't, but maybe my boss will; I'll ask him," replied the young girl.

"Tamara…" the tall, skinny owner of the Dock Side Café queried, scratching his head, and tilting his chef's hat. "I think that's the young lady who always brings her little girl in here. Yeah, she sure does enjoy our special chili dish, and so does the kid. They have a small place not far from here, and it's right on the water. Follow the lakeshore to your right, and the first house with a blue roof; I think that's it, friend."

"Thanks," Zak answered, "and I'll try some of that hot chili."

After finishing his meal, Zak whirled his counter stool around, only to see two overdressed portly men standing beside his Pontiac. Cautiously, he walked from the café and approached the two strangers.

"Anything I can do for you guys?" he asked.

One figure, wearing a long overcoat, smiled. "Yeah, we were just admiring your GTO, friend, it sure is a beauty."

The other stranger, smoking a cigar, walked around the Pontiac to the street side. "My partner's right, this has gotta be worth a good buck." He looked intently into the interior of the car.

Without hesitation, Zak walked deliberately to the driver side, sat behind the wheel, and started the engine. "Not for sale, boys, but keep your eye on the classified pages, I might run a special deal someday."

With both figures standing on each side, the GTO roared between them. Looking in the rear-view mirror,

CHAPTER 15

Zak knew at that moment that the Maniatis gang had continued its relentless search and were not too far away. He purposefully passed the small house with the blue roof, only making note of its location.

Not wanting to involve Sam Rooney's family, Zak decided to drive anywhere through Wayzata, hoping to reach an eventual destination. Spotting a car rental agency, he drove into the opened garage entrance. He screeched to a halt alongside a lineup of rental cars and stepped from the convertible to confront an attendant.

"I need to rent a car for a couple of days," he stated, "and it's worth a couple hundred extra bucks to leave my car here."

The startled employee hesitated, then stammered, "Well, I guess I can make a special arrangement for the right price, if it's only for a day or two."

Driving out of the rental agency in an inconspicuous, grey four-door Chevy wherein he had transferred his gold cache, Zak decided to wait until dark before going to the Tamara home.

At evening time, a short distance from the Tamara home, Zak turned the Chevy headlights off. He pulled up to the white-framed cottage and turned into a narrow side driveway, which ended at the lake's edge. Only a small lamp light brightened the house interior. Stepping through a low picket gate, he rang the doorbell.

The shadow of a woman moved across a curtained window and a young, dark-haired girl stepped onto the screen porch.

"Yes, can I help you?" she asked.

"My name is Zak, and I'm looking for Lisa and Andrew Tamara."

"I'm Lisa Tamara," she quickly replied.

"Lisa, I bring word from your father, Sam Rooney." Zak softly replied.

Her eyes widened and she ran to open the screen door. "Oh, is daddy ok? Is he coming here? Please, do come in, Zak."

Together they entered a tiny living room, where Zak painfully told the detailed story of her father's last hours. Gently touching Lisa's hand, he continued, "Lisa, whatever relationship you and your father shared or didn't share, Sam never stopped thinking of you. Yes, he lived an unexplainable, solitary life, but who are we to judge another's lifestyle, especially if it made him happy. I hardly knew him, Lisa, but we formed a special camaraderie. So much so that I have driven here from California to meet with you and your husband."

CHAPTER 15

Lisa stood up and walked slowly to the kitchen area, bringing a small handkerchief to her face. "Zak, my dad's image and strength never left me. I know he loved me in his strange way, but I wished so much that we, and especially his granddaughter, could have spent some time together." She shook her head, "Would you like some coffee?"

"Sure," Zak faintly replied.

Pouring two cups of coffee and placing them on a small serving table, Lisa began again. "My husband is no longer living with us–my daughter and myself. It's been a few years since he ran off with some bimbo drug companion. They're both presently serving long prison sentences. My daughter, Andrea, and I have made the best of what I suppose could be considered a tough situation. I thank you for coming and letting me know of my father's life, and of his peace now."

Zak moved nervously in the confining wooden chair, "Lisa, there is something else your father practically ordained me to do."

She looked up slowly, a soft look on her face.

"Your father's time wasn't totally wasted," Zak's tone deepened," he amassed a fortune in gold from that High Sierra mine, and it's all bequeathed to you; that's right, gold, and it's all yours."

Lisa rose from her chair, the tiny coffee cup shaking in her hand. "I…I'm not sure you said what I think you did."

Zak stood up. "It's true, Lisa, it's all in the trunk of my car outside, and it rightfully belongs to you and Andrea now."

Lisa held onto a bookcase, her sobs a mixture of joy and sorrow. "Oh, daddy, daddy, how can we ever ask your forgiveness of us, for our long separation, for so many things."

She fell into Zak's arms, and he held her warmly. "Lisa, he's resting in peace now; he told me he would."

"Mommy, Mommy, what's happening? Who is this man?" a small voice from an adjoining bedroom doorway spoke.

"Andrea, sweetheart," implored Lisa, running to her daughter's side, "don't be upset, honey, this is a friend of your grandfather Sam. He's come to help us understand more about Grandpa."

"Hi Andrea, my name is Zak, and I spent some time with your grandfather, way up in the beautiful mountains in California. He would have loved to see you on a pair of kiddie skis up there."

Andrea buried her face into her mother's lap, "We ski here in Minnesota too, Mr. Zak," she countered.

Zak smiled. "I'll bet you do, Andrea, and someday, you'll be covering that downhill territory like an Olympic star."

Sitting back at the coffee table, Zak folded his hands and looked stoically at the mother and daughter. "Lisa, I didn't tell you the whole story," he paused, "there are some people following me—men who could bring harm to me—and I don't want you and Andrea included. I'm certain they also know of the gold, and that makes it more disturbing."

"What does it all mean?" asked Lisa, "what do we do?"

Zak stepped toward them both. "I want both of you to leave with me, tonight and you must leave everything behind. We'll drive to the Minneapolis Airport, where you, your lovely daughter, and the gold will leave for a place, someplace unknown to anyone, even your ex-husband."

Lisa gasped. "Zak…tonight? The airport? Are you crazy?"

Taking her by the shoulders, Zak persisted, "There's no other way, Lisa, time is running out. So help me, if we wait, all I've done to honor your father will be in vain."

HONORING A PROMISE

The big Chevy rental car sped on Interstate Highway 94, towards the airport. Lisa and Andrea sat in the back seat each clutching a small travel bag.

"I'll see to it that the bags of gold are crated, along with your other boxes, and put on a separate cargo plane to your destination," assured Zak.

Breathing heavily, Lisa expressed her concern, "I hope we're doing the right thing, Zak, and I do want you to know that I will do whatever I can to repay you for your kindness."

"There's no need," he replied, "I have the fulfilled a promise I made to your father and that brings me contentment."

"Just get you and Andrea on a big silver bird now and get the heck out of here tonight. With new-found wealth, you can live a life of extraordinary luxury for the rest of your life; now go, quickly."

Arrangements at the busy Minneapolis Airport took on a form of frustrating delays, along with moments of anxiety. Between the swarming crowds at the passenger counters and the slow-moving cargo logistics, Zak suffered trepidation at the thought of being discovered.

Physically rushing Lisa and her daughter up to the very point of final gate departure, Zak breathed in a mild sigh of relief when he watched the 777-jet yaw in a power burst from the runway.

Alone and back in the rental car, racing along the interstate highway, Zak relived the hectic boarding difficulties, especially the separate cargo plane requirements of loading the gold. But most of his frantic hours, he lamented, were spent looking over his shoulder and in every direction for the goons in the big overcoats.

Lisa had given him a forwarding address and the key to her cottage, where he planned to spend the night before turning in the rental car. Making a sharp turn at high speed, he heard a *thump* coming from the back floor area. He swerved to a stop on the highway shoulder and peered over the front seat to see one bag of the gold treasure. It lay half-tilted against the floor hump, a small note attached. Grinning, he realized Lisa had somehow managed to separate one bag of gold for him. He pulled the tiny note pinned to the sack. It read:

> *I know my dad would not want it this way,*
> *especially when he trusted you enough not to*
> *disappear. We trust you, and we wish you warm*
> *winds of safety. We hope to someday meet again.*
> *With Love and Admiration,*
> *Lisa and Andrea*

HONORING A PROMISE

After hiding the gold within the interior panel of the Chevy's trunk, Zak soon arrived at the driveway of Lisa's small, white cottage. After searching each room— including a cramped basement— for possible intrusions, he collapsed upon a provincial sofa in the cozy living room; sleep came gradually.

Awakened by a tickling to his nose, Zak's fuzzy vision caught the bottom edge of a long overcoat. At the coat's upper lapels, a wide, heavy-browed face, covered in cigar smoke and a grin of three gold teeth, growled. "Hey, sleepy head, you was restless, and what's with wearing that Boogey Man hood to bed? You know, Leo and I have the best guaranteed sleeping pill for edgy guys like you."

The intruders laughed, and the terrifying, black circle of a nozzle from a snub nose revolver blocked Zak's view. "Get up, Boogey Man," demanded the gunman.

Sitting up on the sofa, Zak recognized the two large characters he had encountered hanging around his Pontiac GTO at the Lake Side Café. "Better we should introduce ourselves, huh Leo?" the one covering Zak exhorted. "That's Leo the Loony, and I'm Big Georgie," he grinned widely.

Taking initiative, Zak exclaimed, "Well Georgie, Leo, why the gun? What do you want from me?"

Georgie turned around in mock laughter. "Now, ain't that just like a man who has plenty to hide, huh Leo?"

Leo walked over sternly to grab Zak by the shoulders, pulling him up. "Stand up, punk, and take off that hood so we can see who we're talking to."

Zak stood motionless, the dim light reflecting only his piercing eyes within the black shadows of the hood.

"Ok, buster," yelled Leo, "then I'll take it off myself." He roughly grabbed the hood and threw it back. Even the two hoodlums were temporarily transfixed.

"Hey," said Georgie, "now I know why you wear that thing, Boogey Man. I ain't even seen a mug wiped out like that since the Carmen Basilio fight."

"Put the hood back up, dark eyes," winced Leo, "I don't want to look at that face when I do my talking."

Georgie sat down in an old, stuffed chair, waving the snub nose pistol as he spoke. "Let's cut the crap, Boogey Man, Leo, and I can search this joint in half an hour; you can save us all that time. Tell us where the gold is, and hell, we can all go home; we guarantee it."

"Gold?" Zak quizzically interrupted.

"I figured you would say that wise guy," Leo said angrily, "have it your way, dark eyes, and we'll start with giving the basement the once over." He waved the gun, "You lead on, Boogey."

Walking to the basement door, Zak proceeded down a steep staircase, his two captors following closely. Leo flipped a wall switch, dimly lighting the compact chamber. Gas and water pipes hugged a low ceiling, and the cramped interior surprisingly contained an inch or two of water. Georgie pushed his gun barrel against the back of Zak's head.

"Don't try anything down here, dark eyes, or we'll bury you inside that furnace."

"Fellas, I've never seen this leaking basement before in my life," Zak insisted, "so you're wasting your time with me and any notions of gold."

Leo placed his foot into Zak's rear, pushing him to the bottom of the stairs and onto the flooded basement floor.

"Keep up the baloney, dark eyes," Leo growled, "and we'll just take the gold and leave you in the furnace anyway."

Zak pulled himself up to a sitting position on the watery floor. Looking around, he commented, "Looks like this place has some serious seepage from being too close to the lake. Come to think of it, fellas," he smiled, "if there was any gold here, wouldn't your boss Mr. Maniatis want to see it first?"

CHAPTER 15

"Smart guy, ain't he, Leo?" Georgie barked. "Look Boogey man, Leo and I figure Mr. Maniatis and his daughter have enough money. So instead of bringing you to him like he wants, we'll do the asking ourselves and save you the embarrassment of facing the board of directors. Now, get off your butt and stay close between us while we search this dungeon."

A line of two-by-six wood planks were stretched across the floor, obviously placed so that one could avoid stepping in water. It appeared necessary for balance to reach up and hold onto the pipes when walking the narrow beams. Following his hoodlum sentry along a long plank with one foot placed before the other, Zak's arm began to vibrate.

Zak watched Leo and Georgie proceeding ahead of him with their arms raised, holding awkwardly onto the water pipe, and he knew the moment had arrived.

Slowly raising his illuminated left arm, Zak grabbed the overhead pipe. A stream of electrical current flashed through the steel structure in a piercing straight line. The basement light brightened, then went out. A crackling sound erupted against the bubbling of electrified water, and the two burly figures groaned, splashing to the water covered floor. Both overcoats were spread out like tents, covering the grisly, sizzling carnage.

HONORING A PROMISE

After backing out of the cottage driveway in a reverse skid, Zak drove fast, but did not exceed the speed limit to avoid police. Roaring into the car rental agency, he quickly switched the gold to his GTO and sped off. No one at the agency had time to know he had checked in.

CHAPTER 16
THE AGONY OF PURSUIT

Passing the state line of Wisconsin, Zak drove directly due east, hoping to reach the shores of Lake Michigan and eventually make it to Chicago, Illinois. There, perhaps he could lose himself to any pursuers in the vast complexities of the big city. For the moment, it presented a good first stage plan.

Surprised at the ocean-like appearance of Lake Michigan, Zak pulled the green convertible to a halt at a deserted beach ramp. He walked through the sand and soon approached the water's edge. A cool breeze assured the lack of beachcombers. Removing his shoes and socks, he decided to walk and contemplate a permanent escape while strolling the lakeshore.

A myriad of thoughts filled his head while he watched the calm waters trickle through his sinking toes. He had walked a long distance with only an occasional seagull acrobatically darting in front of him. As he looked up and blinked his eyes, a lone figure appeared far up the beach. Unreal at first, the image came toward him.

THE AGONY OF PURSUIT

The figure drew nearer, then faded out, then came back again as it walked the foggy shoreline, mirroring Zak's movements.

He thought it was just a mirage, but the form began to clarify. He considered turning around or walking on an angle toward the beach. He wondered if it could be one of his hunters and questioned if it was foolish to continue. As it came closer, the vague figure solidified into that of a woman.

Zak decided to jog, thinking that if anything unforeseen did occur when their paths met, he would at least be moving. As the woman came into focus, he could see that she was wearing a hooded sweatshirt like his. With both hands in her pockets, she gingerly kicked at the gentle waves. Within twenty feet of one another, neither could see the other's face, and they passed in silence.

Zak breathed a sigh of relief and slowed to a walk when a voice from behind shouted, "Zak, freeze, I've got a gun!"

He halted and turned around slowly to see the woman had pulled back her hood and pointed a gun at him. Long blonde hair waved in the wind against a beautiful oval face, one that he recognized.

"Teresa Maniatis, can it really be you? How in the world did your family find me here?"

She moved carefully toward Zak. "It wasn't easy, Mister Elusive, except when one of our helicopters picked you up on the Wisconsin highway. We do have a modern tracking system today, and I must say, your biggest handicap is that gorgeous hot rod you drive."

"I'm sure with your network of computers, helicopters and informants, anything is possible."

"So don't try anything, Zak, as you can see, I have some assistance coming."

From the highway and onto the beach, two men were running awkwardly through the sand. "Looks like you've decided to join forces with your bad boy father, huh?" Zak said calmly.

Breathing heavily, the two henchmen arrived gasping. "Hey, if it ain't Zorro," barked one, "you sure leave a tough trail, Mr. Weirdo."

The other figure moved up behind Zak, placing a small revolver into his back. "Yeah, and one that's left a trail splattered with cold turkeys—or should I say hot-wired turkeys. Ok, Grim Reaper, don't make any wrong moves, we don't want to join your bloody lineup," demanded the gun totter.

"Leo, Emil," Teresa ordered, "let's bring our man back to the limo. We'll have to go back and search his convertible and drive both cars back to the lodge."

Shuffling through the sand with two guns probing at his back, Zak caustically remarked, "Looks like little Teresa has gone from humility to honcho, eh fellas? Also, I hope someone plans on picking up the shoes I left in the sand."

"Keep walking, Zak," snarled Emil, "we'll keep you barefoot and handicapped."

"Pat him down Emil," Teresa ordered, "we better make sure he isn't carrying a weapon. I've heard too many stories of strange escapes with this guy."

In the limousine, with Emil driving and Zak in the rear seat between him and Teresa, Emil asked, "What's with the electrical gibberish we hear, Zorro? The story goes, a few dudes you encountered died of some crazy bout of lightning or electrical strike; is that a fact?"

Zak remained mute.

Emil continued, "Don't bother me none, Zorro, I never believed in that hokey pokey stuff anyway."

Leo turned from his driving position. "I think you're a real nut, mister, who's playing everybody for a sucker, so watch yourself with us. I plan to keep an eye on your every move, and so help me, I'll blow you away in a wink."

Rounding a gradual curve in the highway, the circular blue and red dome lights of a Wisconsin State trooper car loomed before them. Two troopers were examining the Pontiac GTO abandoned by Zak.

Teresa placed her hands on the back of the right seat. "Leo, drive past the car, we'll have to look for the gold later. Head for the lodge, we can decide later who will come back to pick up the Pontiac," she urged.

They roared past the occupied troopers. "How about my shoes and socks?" Zak complained as they headed for their predetermined lodge.

Resembling a huge, antiquated dance hall, the lodge stood partly on stilts, with a rambling screened-in porch covering the entire exterior. Hanging from the roof rafters on a slight tilt, a faded sign read: "Villa Venice." Extending from the rear of the building, a long white pier canopied the sand and continued far out into the water. Alongside the pier, three expensive cabin cruisers and a small dingy occupied all the slips. A good distance out in Lake Michigan, a sleek, white, and maroon fifty-foot cabin cruiser, tabbed "Myria" lay anchored.

As he walked Zak up the front steps leading to the screened porch, Leo spoke sharply. "We're going to tie your hands, Zak man, with good, old-fashioned rope. We've been told not to use handcuffs because of some cockamamy story of your handcuff magic. Whatever, we're taking no chances; turn around while I tie off your blood flow."

The interior of the lodge portrayed an era gone by, where long ago, flappers of the late 'twenties and men in straw hats and tight suits tripped the light fantastic. A large ballroom, now filled with dinner tables, took up most of the first floor.

"Upstairs, Zorro," ordered Emil, "your room is at the top. You'll have to share it for a while with both Leo and me, if you're not too put out."

Inside a small bedroom, Emil pulled up an antique chair and sat on it backwards. "Ok, Voodoo Man, now's the time to show me some of your magic tricks," he sneered sarcastically.

"I have no magic, Emil, only a hope that somehow, I'll come out of this in one piece. Which makes me wonder, how is it that a woman like Teresa runs the show now? Looks like the old man Phil has turned the reins over to the prettiest one of all."

"Nice try, Zak, but if the Don wants it that way for now, that's the way it'll be," Emil grunted.

"Meaning that you think it's only temporary, Emil?" Zak probed.

Emil grinned. "I know what you're trying to do, hot shot; give it up and get some sleep."

While the other two men snored, Zak spent the long night thinking of a plan to get himself out of this situation.

Early morning winds brought small white caps to the sandy Lake Michigan shore. The boats tied in their slips rocked gently, as though anxious to break away.

As she stood on the long pier, Teresa gave orders. "Leo, I've just talked to my Papa on the ship-to-shore phone. We will take Zak in the dingy to the Myria. We are to rendezvous in deep waters; I have the coordinates. The Don has stated that you, Emil, and I will be held responsible for bringing our prisoner to him."

She quickly walked back toward the lodge. Leo looked at the slinky moves of the slim regimented, often terse lady and thought to himself: *She thinks and talks like her Papa but thank God she does not walk like him.*

On board the luxury cruiser, Emil untied Zak's hands. "Voodoo Man, behave yourself and we can make this trip easy for all of us. For now, relax in one of the deck chairs while my brother, Captain Leo, gets everything shipshape. For me, those fishing rods on the stern are all I need on this tub—which reminds me, we must have thirty pairs of deck shoes on board, pick a pair."

Zak, rubbing his chafed wrists, sat back in a stationary deck chair. "This floating castle you call a tub must sleep twenty."

"Who knows," laughed Emil, "to me it just makes fishing a lot easier."

Powerful marine engines roared to life, swirling a turbulence of white water from beneath the glistening stern.

From the modern, fully equipped fly bridge, Leo shouted, "Ok, land lubbers, hold fast; were heading for open water, which looks a little rough right now. Emil, see that the magician doesn't commit suicide by going overboard."

The rakish cruiser, with its state-of-the-art radar and sonar configurations, rose in the water and powered forward into a morning mist. On the bridge, Teresa's flowing blonde hair streaked across her beautiful icy features. Soon the shoreline faded from sight. The big boat knifed smoothly through the deep purple and blue waters on Lake Michigan.

Zak reached for one of the guest fishing rods. "Am I correct in assuming we might be heading for a meeting with the top man himself?" he asked.

CHAPTER 16

Emil, casting a line from a high, swivel deck chair, smiled. "Mr. M does like to get to open waters once in a while. But don't let it get to you now, Voodoo Man; grab that new graphite rod and enjoy the fishing."

Standing on opposite sides of the rear deck casting their fishing rods into the choppy water, Zak realized the jolting tremor in his energized arm.

"Hey, Captain Leo, slow down a little—my line runs out too fast," Emil yelled.

Zak looked down at his high-test steel line wrapped tightly around a highly efficient reel. His electric hand had transformed the line into a live wire. In one left wrist motion, he whipped his electrified fishing line toward Emil, crackling like a whip.

Arching across the deck, the electrified line snaked around the heavy neck of Emil. Zak jerked his rod slightly and a *zap* sound lifted Emil from his feet, and in a flash, flipped him overboard; he never made a sound. Zak let the fishing line run furiously to its end, then Emil's weight pulled the rod with him into the water.

Alone on the boat's fan tail, his arm crackling with bright colors of bluish-white and purple, Zak pondered his next move. His instincts quickly directed him to four steps leading to the lower cabin compartment. There, a lineup of expensive bric-a-brac adorned a mahogany interior. Lavish sleeping quarters adjoined by a unique, scaled down kitchen arrangement lined the bow area. Careful not to touch any conductive material with his insurgent arm, Zak looked around for a gun.

From the bridge, Leo shouted, "Hey Emil, get me and Teresa some wine, and see what else is in the refrigerator, will ya?"

Zak froze, knowing Leo or Teresa would soon investigate.

The galley contained an array of utensils, including knives and even a meat cleaver. Zak placed a long knife into his belt. Two oval Persian rugs covered the kitchen floor. He kicked aside both rugs, revealing a wooden grate set in the floor. Pulling the grate up, he saw enough room to hide.

"Hey Emil, I got this thing on auto pilot," came the gruff voice of Captain Leo, "I'm coming down."

In seconds, he poked his head and a large caliber gun nozzle cautiously into the cabin compartment. "Emil, what's going on, brother?" he continued, "what the heck happened to Voodoo Man, where are you bro?"

Leo stepped slowly into the kitchen area. "Ok, magician, I get the message," he demanded, "but I also have the fire power, wise guy. Don't be stupid, Voodoo Man, show me my brother and step out." But only the slow, methodical purr of the cruiser's mellow engines could be heard.

In the dimly lit cabin, Leo called out to Teresa, "Teresa, if you can, you better come down here quick with a gun."

Then, his eyes caught the flashing of a strange blue light streaming from under the floor grate. Bending down for closer observation, his fingers gnarled around the wooden squares, but Zak's fingers enveloped his. The cabin quarters filled with a jolting sound and an eye-blinding glow; Leo gasped and made a gurgling sound. His body stiffened and he sprawled out, filling the narrow galley.

Pushing against the floor grate and Leo's body weight, Zak squeezed from his hiding place, his electric arm diminishing. Now, only him and Teresa were aboard the rolling, fifty-foot boat, cruising through the vast Lake Michigan waters.

Zak scampered to the cabin floor and cautiously looked toward the fly bridge. He could not see or hear Teresa. He winced when suddenly, the engines ceased. The extraordinary cabin cruiser eased back into the heavier rocking motions of the open water. Only a creaking of the boat's superstructure broke the eerie stillness.

Breaking the silence, Teresa's strong voice prevailed, "Zak, Zak, I don't know what happened to Leo or Emil, but wherever you are, you should know I can pilot this boat. I'm well versed in navigational training, and I have an automatic weapon. It would be better, Zak, for you to come forward and negotiate." The silence continued.

Slowly, Zak walked out into full view to stand on the open lower deck. "Ok, Teresa, perhaps under the circumstances, we can talk. Considering your father is waiting for us—— or more importantly, me, alive, let's discuss the situation."

Teresa, cradling an Uzi automatic gun, stepped warily down the few stairs leading from the bridge. "Zak, are Leo and Emil on board, or—"

"—They're not on board," Zak interrupted.

Teresa's ashen face twisted. "How…what did you do to them? Where are they?" She could not see Zak's face, concealed totally by a strong wind at his back that pushed the ski hood forward.

"Your friends have taken to the deep," Zak explained.

The Myria began to flounder, throwing Teresa against the stair railing and Zak against the deck rail.

"Well, Teresa—or should I call you Godmother, or whatever it is you call a female mob chieftain."

"My father is in charge of the organization, and you know it," she shot back.

"For now," Zak countered, "as long as his poor health holds out."

Teresa, releasing her hold on the railing, moved to the deck to sit at a small metal table anchored to the floor. She placed the Uzi on the table and aimed it at Zak.

"My position as second in command is a matter of family heritage," she insisted.

With his hands raised, Zak asked if he could sit at an opposite chair; Teresa nodded yes. "Tell me, Teresa," Zak's features tightened, "what do you think your father will do when he finds out you killed his two sons—your own brothers—for the sake of heritage?"

Teresa did not reply, her cold composure mirroring that of her father's. "You do what you must do in this business, Mr. Zak. Too bad you figured that out, my dark friend. Come to think of it, my father would understand how I had to kill you during a struggle with Leo and Emil, and how you all took an unfortunate plunge into the deep water. For your information, Zak, my father has always believed you were part of the conspiracy which killed my brothers."

"Only one thing you forgot, Teresa," Zak pronounced stoically, "something everyone has been telling you about me."

She looked at him dumbfounded.

"My weird electric arm," he proceeded, "and how it is especially conductive to metal, like this table and the steel Uzi resting on it."

Instantly, an electrical neon rim encircled the table, the Uzi, and Teresa. She screamed, stiffened, and violently spun to the deck in a ring of smoke. Zak slowly toppled from his chair to sit on the deck. He stayed there for a while before gently picking up Teresa's singed body. Placing her still warm remains in a small white tarp, he presented it overboard.

Zak made his way to the stairway and continued up to the flying bridge. Examining the boat's complex instrument panel, he managed to restart the twin engines and control the boat's navigational system. The compass data enabled him to come around and head west. Through an onboard computer, he soon set an auto pilot reckoning back to their original port.

Visibility turned clear upon approaching land and he pulled anchor a good half mile from the shore. The old Villa Venice Ballroom could be seen close offshore. He clamored over the elegant cruiser railing and made his way in the motorized dingy, hoping to come ashore close to where he parked the GTO. Running the dingy around, Zak splashed his way ashore, grinning when he saw his shoes and socks still intrenched in the sand. After snapping up his shoes, he ran full gait in the direction of his Pontiac sanctuary. A feeling of relief engulfed him when the silhouette of the green convertible came into view.

A thin coat of sand covered the leather convertible top and the windows appeared streaked and dirty. Plastered on the passenger side window, an orange police warning sticker related the message of impending removal. He took a deep breath upon turning the ignition key and enjoyed the instant blast of the familiar high-performance engine.

Following the shoreline highway, thoughts of his precarious journey and being followed by relentless pursuers returned to plague him. With the obvious triple tragedy of today, he now represented the mob's personal public enemy number one. Zak knew the deaths, especially of Teresa, sealed his doom.

Could he ever get away? Could there be a way to avoid the inevitable, the resigned wrath of the mob to eliminate him? From the stories he had read, some tried, but none succeeded.

THE AGONY OF PURSUIT

Looking up at the small St. Jude medal he had hung over the rearview mirror, he prayed aloud. "Well, Saint of Lost Causes, this one would test even your miracles."

CHAPTER 17
A BLUEPRINT FOR
SURVIVAL

Passing through the prestigious northern suburbs that lined Chicago's picturesque lakefront, Zak soon arrived in Chicago. He thought Chicago's skyline needed mountains. With snowcapped mountains behind the Windy City's extraordinary skyscrapers, he mused, California might have tough competition. He decided to scrap the decision to hide in the dark recesses of the big city, but to in fact take the reverse course of being accessible in one of Chicago's top hotels.

Maniatis might not think he could be so brash, so stupid as to avail himself openly at Chicago's posh Marriot or Hyatt or Drake Hotel, Zak reasoned. His inner conscious mulled; Maniatis dislikes the crowds, the lights. The idea of too much publicity, too many police, is taboo to the usual secrecy the mob prefers, a slim chance, but worth the try.

After parking the Pontiac in an underground public garage, Zak opened the vehicle's inner door panel to remove the gold from inside. Placing it in a small duffel bag, he ran from the garage, hailed a taxi, and asked the cabby to take him to the Marriott Hotel. He secured a fashionable suite on the top floor and threw himself upon a satin-covered, oversize bed. After restlessly twisting and turning, he fell asleep.

An anguished night of flashing dreams included a multi-colored, photo film treadmill passing beneath his jogging feet. A cinema of past events rushed before him in panoramic proportions. One image appeared in recurrent vignettes: Sister Julie.

At noon, Zak awoke with a slight headache. Oddly, he found himself sprawled on the floor entangled with blankets; it seemed he had fallen out of bed without waking up. He unraveled the satin spread as he slowly turned his feet.

Even sleep can prove exhausting, he thought.

Sitting back on the bed, he pulled down the cumbersome hood from his face. As he grabbed the back of his neck to massage a muscle spasm, he considered calling St. James Hospital in Nevada. It would be comforting to know about Sister Julie's recovery and whereabouts.

Using the bed stand phone, he finally contacted St. James Hospital after several disconnections. Sister Julie had recovered well, and fortunately had left a message with the hospital administration regarding her reassignment to a Catholic seminary in St. Charles, Illinois.

"What a stroke of luck!" he exclaimed, "she's close by in Illinois."

Leafing through the Chicago phone directory, Zak found the Belle Armaine Seminary listing. Hesitantly, he dialed the number, wondering if Sister Julie would be receptive to his call. A Mother Amadeus of the seminary answered. She informed Zak that a small group, including Sister Julie, were attending a children's mission gathering at McCormick Place in downtown Chicago.

On Chicago's Michigan Avenue, Zak waited to catch a taxi. He noticed a barrage of police cars speeding along "The Magnificent Mile," their flashing dome lights seemingly everywhere.

Once he finally waved down a taxi, Zak opened the car door. "Driver, what's with the squad cars?" he asked the driver.

"Someone told me a couple of kids tried to steal a classic sports car in the city's underground garage," he replied. "The damn car blew up like an atom bomb when they crossed the wires; crazy ain't it?"

Zak slowly sunk into the cab seat. He realized the obvious—the mob had found his GTO and planted an explosive.

So much for my stupid idea of diverting Philip Maniatis. The poor dumb thieves: those kids sure picked the wrong car to try and steal.

Shortly, the cab pulled alongside the lakefront exposition center. Inside the mammoth edifice, a wall directory indicated the Belle Armaine Children's Charity Bash. Proceeding to a long escalator, he soon found the small glassed-in room containing a religious order of women.

As he surveyed the group of extremely conservatively dressed educators, his eye caught the unquestionable serene beauty of Sister Julie. Attired in black with a touch of grey and trimmed by a small white collar, her natural radiance glowed in contrast.

At the top of the escalator, well in view of the meeting room door, Zak waited nervously. When the door opened and the women streamed out in his direction, he could see Sister Julie involved in earnest conversation.

Zak walked tentatively toward her, and as she casually looked up, her eyes widened.

"Zak, Zak, can it be you?" she exclaimed.

"Sister Julie," Zak replied, "I can't tell you how great it is to see you again; you look beautiful."

Blushing as her companions shied away from the encounter, Sister Julie took Zak's hands. "Zak, my dear friend, I had hoped so much to see you again." After an uncomfortable momentary pause, she continued, "How did you ever find me here?"

Zak smiled. "Is there a coffee shop in this place, Sister? Maybe you could spare some time?"

"By all means," she answered, "our meetings are over until tomorrow morning, and I'd love some coffee; follow me."

Seated at a small circular glass table within an atmosphere of manicured plants and a massive French window overlooking Lake Michigan, they shared a special reunion.

Sister Julie sipped on a cup of coffee. "This is unbelievable," she said, "how did you get here, what has occurred since St. James Hospital?"

Zak held up two hands, "Hold it, Sister, that's a long story and frankly, it's too complex to live again."

"You mean things have been difficult?" she asked.

Zak smiled. "Sister, I've come here to find out about you, about your recovery, your present situation, and everything else. I can't explain my being here, except I just wanted to see you again. To know that you were ok, and yes, to find out about your official status. I guess I mean, have you ever confirmed those religious commitments?"

Sister Julie beamed. "My recovery has been swift, and I thank you for helping me on that. I guess with the disappearance of those cumbersome religious habits, and our present non-descript grey suits, most people wonder if I'm a nun or not. Actually, my final vows take place the first Sunday of next month. It has taken me awhile to realize that I will probably never be certain. The truth is my eternal labor of love, and my prayers will assist me in times of doubt. Right now, that's what I want most of all."

"I'm happy for you," assured Zak, "but, and forgive me for being direct, perhaps I wanted to see you again to let you know that someone cared. In fact, someone hoped you might change your mind."

She coyly responded, "Zak, I think we both knew…" her voice trailed. "I shall never forget or regret those intimate moments we shared in the mountains. What we enjoyed, I admit, has oftentimes conjured up memories and confused my dedication. But…" she paused, "what is it Zak, why do you look toward the windows so often?"

"Sorry, Sister," Zak apologized, "I just wonder about those two men seated near the French windows."

CHAPTER 17

Zak stood up. "Am I paranoid, or do they look out of place to you in their shiny dark suits?"

Sister Julie looked in the direction of the two figures. "I really don't know what you mean, Zak, they are simply enjoying a meal as far as I can see. Why, are you in danger? Are you being followed?"

She leaned over the table. "Zak, perhaps you can forgive me, but I wanted to ask you about your evasive manner. Including the hood you always wear to shroud your obscured face. Surely, I'm not being presumptuous?"

Zak reached across the table to take her hand. "It's a paranoia, a facial disfigurement, and that is a long story. I'm sorry for my obvious clandestine ways and apprehensions, but there have been many unfortunate occurrences—too many to cover now. They are left for me to solve, and not for you to concern yourself with."

"Whatever, I just hate to see you so anxious," she expressed warily.

They both attempted a smile. "I would like you to come with me now," Sister Julie stated, "to see our giant toy box; it's part of the Children's Charity Bash we dreamed up."

Pulling Zak in the direction of the meeting room, together they scurried into the small quarters—but not before Zak glanced back in the direction of the two characters. At one end of the room, a huge red box the size of a small car filled half the room. Extra big rainbow-colored letters read: "Toy Bash." Sister Julie lifted the lid of the heavy box, revealing enough toys to fill a toy store.

"Wow," Zak exclaimed, "I would have liked to live in that box as a kid."

Suddenly, both were stunned by the loud sound of a thud. A heavy .357 Magnum revolver landed in the toy box on top of a red wagon. Turning in terror, they saw a short, thin man with a handlebar mustache wearing a dark, satin-textured grey suit.

Through a muffled laugh, the intruder spoke. "I hope you get the message; it's either toys or noise, Dark Specter—take your pick. Lady, I trust you'll accept my donation to all the kiddies, only, it ain't a toy."

A second, much taller man stood in the doorway, his black, shiny suit covering the entrance.

The mustached one maintained a smirk, keeping his hands in his suit pockets as he talked. "Like I said, Mr. Specter, you come with us, and the lady stays with her play toys. No trouble, no nothing, and everybody comes out like a happy Jack-in-the-Box; sound like a fair deal?"

Zak looked at Sister Julie. "How do I know you'll let her go?"

Continuing his twisted facial grin, the short one walked to the toy box to retrieve his gun. "We came for you, mystery man, and only you. The orders came from the top, and they don't include a broad. So, play it cool, walk backwards toward my partner, and we'll leave together peacefully and quietly, you got it? Your girlfriend, she has a nice face, let's leave it that way."

Walking backward as instructed, Zak quietly assured Sister Julie, "I'll be alright, Sister, only if you promise not to follow us. I must know you'll think of the children and let me go with these men quietly."

"I'll do as you say, Zak," Sister Julie whispered almost inaudibly. She watched in horror as the two thugs rustled Zak down a long hallway leading to the escalator.

Hyperventilating, Sister Julie staggered from the meeting room. After fighting to gain some stability, she ran to the nearest security guard to relate the harrowing abduction. While the guards formed and then dispersed, she ran to the west side of the building bordering Lake Shore Drive.

There, she looked out the big window at a sea of cars jamming the famous Outer Drive. "Oh Zak," she muttered, "you made yourself vulnerable by coming to see me; may God be with you."

A BLUEPRINT FOR SURVIVAL

Inside a black stretch limousine that was specially equipped to rope their captive to a small jump seat, Zak sat pensively. The jump seat, situated between the middle and front seats, afforded his three captors—including the driver—close observance.

Unexpectedly, A Chicago Bear's football preseason game had just finished nearby at Soldier Field Stadium. Jammed traffic on the winding Lake Shore Drive lined north and south as far as the eyes could see.

"Unbelievable," the chauffeur driver snarled, "what a bad break, a football game! We're stopped cold, Ed, there's no way out of this."

Ed, the mustached one, rolled down the electric window. "Relax, Charlie, no one is going anywhere, including the police. Follow the crowd and we'll be at O'Hare Airport in no time.

Edging their way in a mass of cars that resembled a cattle drive, the limo finally reached the entrance to the Eisenhower Expressway. Heading west, they gradually picked up speed as the traffic dilemma slowly cleared. Ed and his partner stared intently at Zak, and no one spoke a single word.

CHAPTER 18
DESPERATE HOURS

The long silence prevailed inside the stretch limousine. While they jockeyed through flowing traffic, a fender bender accident a few blocks ahead brought their car to a gradual stop.

"This dirty bottleneck city is going to drive me nuts," grumbled Charlie, the chauffeur.

Soon, they approached some wild pedestrians that were walking on the expressway, singing, and weaving through the stalled vehicles. Two colorfully dressed youngsters approached the limousine, spewing vulgar language and pounding on the hood.

"Hey, man, what's with the black beauty Cadillac jiving with you slugs?" yelled one.

The two characters unexpectedly opened the limo doors before anyone could react.

One boy, wearing a baseball cap and holding a small automatic weapon, shouted, "Ok, dudes, this is the end of the line. What you all call carjacking city is upon you. So stay cool, ugly, you know what I mean."

"Everybody hit the street, or we make you meat, you hear me, dudes?" his cohort hollered.

Fiercely brandishing their automatic firepower, they forced the mobsters to abandon the limousine.

Ed attempted a remark. "Listen, kids, you're messing with more than you can—"

"—Jam it, dude," the baseball-capped one cut him off, "or I'll dirty your fancy pants with your own guts. Sit down on the guard rail, fat boy."

In fear and frustration, the three mobsters walked begrudgingly to the guard rail.

As they stood on both sides of the limo, the carjackers realized that one occupant remained in the back seat.

"Hey, Momo," shouted one, "get the guy with the straight jacket, man."

The one called Momo grabbed Zak by the shoulders and attempted to drag him from the car. "Man, this dude is cemented to this love boat."

"Cut him bad, Momo, and rip him out; I'll give you a hand," laughed the baseball-capped punk.

From their vantage point at the guard rail, the mobsters observed a blinding blue light fill the interior of the limousine, accompanied by a cracking sound and two long screams. Astonished by what they saw, the three hoodlums stood, unable to move.

CHAPTER 18

Other cars with distressed occupants pulled around the smoking limousine. Slowly, Ed and Ziggy walked back to examine their vehicle. Curling smoke streamed from the opened doors. They cautiously peered inside.

Both carjackers were bent over in a crumpled heap, their colorful clothes now totally blackened.

"It stinks like burnt flesh in here," Ed remarked in his gravelly voice.

Inside the limo, Zak sat motionless as he faced forward, his once roped arms free from the special restraints. The bulky hood partially covered his impassioned face.

Charlie, the chauffeur, stood frozen, his eyes glued to Zak. He then looked at his partners, said nothing, and turned to flee along the guard rail. He fell twice, recovered, and fled into the jungle of stalled traffic.

"Charlie, Charlie," cried Ed, but to no avail. He whirled around, confronting Zak with the revolver. "I don't know what the heck all this is about, mystery man, but we've got to get out of here, fast." He pointed to his partner. "Ziggy, you tie his hands again really good and drive off this expressway. We'll dump these crazy kids later."

The oversized limousine slowly zagged its way through the traffic and soon exited at an off-ramp.

"Ziggy," Ed growled, "head for an alleyway or an empty building where we can get rid of this smelly baggage."

Jamming the gun into Zak's shadowed face, he continued. "I'm only going to say this once, Houdini. A twitch of your finger, and so help me, I'll blow your brains all over this back seat. How you torched these punk kids means we could whack you now, without a Maniatis order; you got me?"

As they turned into a cluttered alley, the bright headlight beams startled a scattering of rats and revealed an array of debris and overstuffed garbage cans. Stopping alongside an abandoned truck garage, Ziggy and Ed dragged the smoldering bodies of the young carjackers inside the open structure.

Their job complete, they drove on, meandering through a blight of poverty-strewn neighborhoods. Finally, Ziggy managed to find an entrance ramp back to the expressway.

As they approached O'Hare International Airport, Ziggy looked into the rearview mirror. "Ed, we're only ten minutes from O'Hare; shoot that crazy pyro if he looks cross-eyed," he warned.

Once they entered the ticket gate at the O'Hare parking facility, the shiny Cadillac whirled up the circular ramps, wasting no time stopping at the first available birth. Grappling with their captive, Ed and Ziggy yanked Zak from his bondage. They proceeded up an elevator to the fourth floor and roughly herded him into a room marked "Employees Only."

The small, brightly lit crew quarters contained only a small table and a smattering of ashtrays surrounded by six chairs. Ed quickly tied Zak to a chair, using enough rope to cover half of his body.

"This makes me feel better, Mr. Dark Storm," Ziggy grumbled, "I only hope one of the bosses gets here fast."

Both mobsters sat at the table, and in cadence, lit their cigarettes. Heavy smoke swirled across their strained faces. Conversation ceased, as Ed and Ziggy could only stare menacingly at their quiet, spooky prisoner.

When the metal door partially opened, an obese man wearing a semi-tuxedo entered with a broad smile on his face. "Hey Ziggy, Big Ed," he blurted and extended a short, stubby handshake to his mob affiliates. Ed and Ziggy quickly returned to their felicitations.

Suddenly, the door swung fully open, revealing the mob czar Philip Maniatis sitting in his perennial wheelchair, awkwardly navigating the cramped quarters.

Ed stood up. "Mr. M, we weren't sure you would be here in Chicago; it's good to see you."

Ziggy nodded. "Yeah, boss, we had a rough go with this oddball here, but we got him as promised; and on time."

Philip Maniatis, haggard, remained placid while he slowly moved around the table, pushing buttons on the electronic wheelchair to confront Zak. He spoke in staccato, "Well, Mr. Mirage, we meet again. Only this time, I'm minus two sons and a loving daughter."

A long, uncomfortable pause ensued. Maniatis' voice wavered, "There is a rage inside of me with your name on it."

Zak looked straight forward, the ski hood darkening most of his tense face as usual. "The story is a long one, Maniatis. Too long to tell now, and probably one you wouldn't believe anyway."

Pushing the forward on the wheelchair to its limit, Maniatis banged the chair into Zak's legs. The button noise continued to sound. His black eyes glaring, the mob boss yanked back Zak's hood. The scarred, deformed face lay open for the shocked observers.

"Get this monster son of a bitch on his feet now and to my plane within fifteen minutes!" Maniatis hollered. "I want him back in Vegas; this will be my retribution, nice and slow, a crowning achievement to my family. I promise you, Zak, your body will be harder to find than Jimmy Hoffa's."

Maniatis lowered his head and gripped his wiry greyish black hair. "Get him out of my sight," he demanded.

DESPERATE HOURS

CHAPTER 19
A JOURNEY INTO OBLIVION

Escorting Zak through several isolated terminals, the three gangsters hustled him onto a private aircraft zone. On the tarmac, a modern, French-designed DeHavelin Jet waited. Using the cover of darkness, the three captors jostled Zak up a portable ramp that led to their boss's sleek silver and black aircraft.

They entered the plane's plush cabin, where Philip Maniatis sat at a small cocktail bar, a tall scotch and water in his hand.

"Bring him to the back, as far away from me as possible," Maniatis ordered, "and all of you leave too. Except for the flight crew, I want to be alone with this miscarriage."

His subordinates followed his instructions and tied Zak to a rear seat before exiting the plane just as quickly as they entered.

A uniformed pilot emerged from the cockpit door. "Mr. Maniatis, we're cleared to proceed to runway 42L if you're ready."

"Captain Lagos, I'm ready when you are," Maniatis affirmed without hesitation.

The small, but highly efficient DeHavelin soon rocketed from the runway in a spectacular roar. Once the aircraft swiftly reached cruising altitude at 34,000 feet, Maniatis resumed drinking at the custom-made bar. A padded wall displaying pop art shielded him from seeing Zak, but he rambled on, nevertheless.

"Zak is what they call you, eh? Well, Mr. Zak, you've given us a murderous chase. I paid dearly for that long run of carnage with the lives of my whole life—my children."

"We only have one bag of gold from your hotel room," he continued, "we'll get the rest. But right now, I don't care about gold; I only care about my forever remembered family. That's why I'm taking you back to Las Vegas with me. I have big plans for you, Mr. Zak, the biggest ever."

"I don't imagine it's a party or something I can send my regrets to," Zak interjected. "But you should know that I had nothing to do with the assassinations of your sons or the death of your daughter. Also— and I hope you can handle this—your lovely daughter actually planned her brothers' funerals and mine too. Whatever tragedy happened between your daughter and me came down to kill or be killed."

Maniatis gulped down another glass of scotch and water and coughed, struggling to speak through an obvious spasm. "You lying, no-good bastard. You hide from the truth, just like you hide your face."

The rakish silver bird streaked through the vacuum-clear sky, climbing to 37,000 feet on a course due west.

"Weather is crystal clear all the way," the pilot's intercom announced.

Maniatis poured another mixed drink, spilling some on his unique bar. He then rolled his wheelchair down the specially made aisle to hold court with Zak. "A couple more hours, Dark One, and the Nevada desert will prove you can bury something in its sand forever. In the meantime, why don't you pull back your hood; you can relax and enjoy my big bird, and what's left of your short life."

Zak looked directly at Maniatis, partially uncovering his crippled face. "I prefer to hide what some would call a gruesome kisser, Maniatis, but you're right about this silver kite; it's sonic cool. I noticed you have a parachute in the opened closet; what's that all about?"

Maniatis gulped down a good swig of scotch. "That's for me, hotshot. I'm superstitious, and yes, I hate flying.

This is probably the only supersonic private jet with an old-fashioned parachute. My baby has all the latest scientific technology and is, in fact, a scaled-down version of the best commercial aircraft—except for my personal safety net."

Zak smiled, and a whisper of scorn crossed his face. "How about that? The tough, powerful kingpin of the Vegas gambling empire, afraid to fly."

Maniatis rolled unsteadily back toward the bar again. "Sure, and some say I drink too much, but they never say it to my face. So, Mr. Shadow, how about one last drink for my most hated enemy. Maybe even a sick statement to your most dastardly deed, the murder of my loved ones."

His wheelchair bumped violently into the partitioned wall, almost throwing Maniatis to the floor.

Pressing the correct wheelchair buttons, he proceeded to the bar. "That drunk driving calls for a drink too," he slurred.

"We will be over the Sierra Nevada in just a few minutes, Mr. Maniatis," squeaked the voice from the cockpit's intercom.

Zak looked out the small window at the gigantic, snow-capped mountains profiled against the black sky.

CHAPTER 19

His memory drifted back to the electrical wire incident, Sam Rooney, and Sister Julie.

Funny, he thought, *if I had been afraid of heights, storms, or lightning, this whole thing may never have happened.*

A billion stars blanketed the stark, clear night over the Nevada desert. The tiny jet stream from the glistening airplane went unnoticed in the majestic, cloudless dark sky.

Two old-timers camping near the base of the High Sierras quickly looked up. "Golly gee, if that don't look like a meteorite or a comet!" one shouted.

From the sky, an electrical explosion, followed by a blazing, arch-like trail, resembled a falling star plummeting toward Earth. Only the final, fiery explosion atop the mountains gave signs of an airplane crash.

Two days later, a tired search team reached the summit and found the charred, entangled wreckage of the newest DeHavelin jet. Newspaper reports rapidly spread news that the big Las Vegas chieftain was found dead, along with the flight crew, in the cremated fuselage.

Standing amidst the still simmering junk pile of aircraft debris, one scorched rescuer turned to his companion. "Fred, the one thing I can't figure out is that witnesses reported seeing lightning. Can you imagine that? Lightning! And there were no storms within a five-state area."

"Yeah," his partner replied, "and you won't believe this, but one seasoned camper, who probably had one six-pack of beer too many, said that he spotted, of all things—"

His friend interrupted, "—What?"

Fred shook his head. "A parachute."

The End

ABOUT THE AUTHOR

Budd Steadman (1929-2021) was an American author, and *The Man with the Electric Arm* was his first novel. Steadman was a Shakespeare enthusiast and gifted artist, and wrote and illustrated several novels, books, and short stories. *The Man with the Electric Arm* was his first and signature novel.

Steadman's legacy is carried on through his children, his grandchildren, and his writings, which are being exclusively published by No Limit Enterprises, Inc. Steadman lived and worked in Chicago, Illinois, United States.